MW01128690

CHRISTMAS WISH

A HOLIDAY ROMANCE NOVEL

AMANDA SIEGRIST

Copyright © 2018 Amanda Siegrist
All Rights Reserved.

This material may not be re-produced, re-formatted, or copied in any format for sale or personal use unless given permission by the publisher.

All characters in this book are a product of the author's imagination. Places, events, and locations mentioned either are created to help inspire the story or are real and used in a fictitious manner.

Note: The towns mentioned in this story are fictitious, except for St. Cloud. That is a real city in Minnesota full of culture, beauty, and kindness. You should visit it someday.

Cover Designer: Amanda Siegrist
Photo Provided by: 4 PM Production/Shutterstock.com
Edited by: Nadara "Nay" Merrill - www.thatgrammargal.com

ALSO BY AMANDA SIEGRIST

A happy ending is all I need.

Holiday Romance Novel

Merry Me

Mistletoe Magic

Snowed in Love

Snowflakes and Shots

Holiday Hope

McCord Family Novel

Protecting You

Trust in Love

Deserving You

Always Kind of Love

Finding You

Perfect For You Novel

The Wrong Brother

The Right Time

The Easy Part

The Hard Choice

Standalone Novel

The Danger with Love

Lucky Town Novel

Escaping Memories

Dangerous Memories

Stolen Memories

Deadly Memories

One Taste Novel

One Taste of You

One Taste of Love

One Taste of Crazy

One Taste of Sin

One Taste of Redemption

One Taste of Hope

Conquering Fear Novel

Co-written with Jane Blythe

Drowning in You

Out of the Darkness

Merry Christmas.

May your days and nights be filled with holiday cheer!

A Special Note...

I love writing flash fiction! I absolutely adore it. It really gets the ideas flowing. This story started out right away with a flash scene. I had no idea how it would start, and bam! Someone gave me a prompt and I decided to use it with my Christmas story. A few scenes were written with flash prompts. It will be noted at the beginning of chapter one and chapter nine, just for your information, if you happen to be curious. *chuckles*

♥ Much love, Amanda Siegrist

1

WRITING PROMPTS: IT'S TOO HOT. I HATE HATS. THE RED STAPLER.

He grabbed the dog by the scruff of his neck and cradled him as close to his chest as he could, shielding him from the burning inferno. The heat scorched him straight through his gear, so he could just imagine how the dog felt. Puppy, more like it. Unless it was one of those tiny dogs that people loved to dress up and put in designer purses and do a number of frivolous stuff with. He honestly had no clue. All he knew were the cries of the little girl screaming for her dog had him running back in the house.

Probably the dumbest thing he could've done.

Heat was coming from all directions. The flames licked at his body. The smoke mixed in didn't help him to see a clear path out of the house that was sure to crumble at any moment.

So dumb. All for an animal.

But he would've never been able to live with himself knowing he didn't at least make an effort for the little girl.

Crouching low as he walked down what he assumed was the hallway, he tried to keep his sanity as the flames seared his backside. If he made it out of this house with half his body coated in burns, he wouldn't be shocked.

His muscles started to get heavy, his breathing labored, even with his mask on and the oxygen flowing nicely.

"It's too hot." He squeezed the dog reassuringly. "But I'm going to get you out of here."

Every time he turned his head, trying to get his bearings down, all he saw was orange and red. Bright flames waiting to fry him like a hot dog over an open fire pit.

"Bentley. To your right."

The sound of his buddy talking in his ear sent a rush of hope straight to his veins. Like a shot of adrenaline. He had no idea what was to his right. More flames? More heat? More smoke? Freedom? He didn't care. His fellow firefighter said to turn right, so he was going to turn right.

Making the turn as fast as he could, the dog still clutched tightly in his arms, he didn't pause as his buddy grabbed his arm and led him out of the house via the back door. Which was crazy, because he remembered entering the house through the front door. Searching for the dog and then attempting to find his way out had really turned him around.

After getting far away from the house, he collapsed to the ground, set the dog down gently, who barely moved, and shoved off his helmet and mask, gulping in a huge breath of fresh air.

"That was a close one, man. I can't believe you went back in."

Bentley took another huge breath of air, then grinned at Charlie, his savior. "I had to get the dog. He's a part of their family." He looked down at the dog, who sat quietly by his side, his soulful eyes glancing up at him as if he understood what just happened.

The dog was safe. The little girl would be happy. Nothing else mattered.

Charlie clapped him on the back and chuckled. "You're crazy sometimes. Glad you're okay."

"Thanks for coming in for me."

"Always."

Charlie scooped up the dog and walked away. Bentley smiled as he heard the delightful squeals from the little girl as she grabbed her precious pet.

It was a puppy. A small golden retriever that would live to see another day.

Because of him.

He couldn't wait to get home, take a shower, grab a beer, and appreciate the silence for once. The fact he ran into a burning home that was ready to fall apart at any moment and saved a dog because a little girl pleaded for him to do so made him feel grateful to be alive.

Thinking about it now, it had been a dumb decision to run back in the house. But it all worked out.

Standing up, he tried not to imagine how badly the fire chief would ream him out for his reckless actions.

He walked to the front of the house, where the rest of the crew battled the flames, and went right to the chief, who had a fierce expression on his face.

"We'll talk later. You hurt?"

Bentley shook his head. "Not a scratch." Shockingly. Because he swore he felt the flames blazing right through his turnout jacket.

"Why are you still standing around?"

He shoved his helmet on his head and jumped back in to help his fellow firefighters tame the fire burning through the Daughtry's family home.

They'd snuff this fire out, but it didn't matter. Besides the barn standing tall and proud behind them, the house was a complete loss.

Christmas was only two and a half weeks away. What a way to spend the holidays. Homeless.

As he grabbed part of the hose behind Charlie, he couldn't help but remember what happened to Theresa's home last Christmas. Theresa was his best friend's wife. He knew as soon as she found out, as well as most of the other townsfolk, the Daughtry's wouldn't feel homeless. The town would band together and make sure they had the best damn Christmas they could this year.

Because that's what they did in Mulberry. They looked out for each other.

He knew exactly who'd be at the center of the organization to turn their crappy holiday into a beautiful one.

Daphne.

The one woman he let get away. The one woman he would never have.

She was getting married in two and a half weeks. On Christmas Eve.

The Daughtry's might still have a wonderful holiday.

But for him—this Christmas was going to suck.

HER FINGERS CURLED around the door handle, and with one quick breath, she pulled it open. There was nothing to be nervous about. Nothing. She didn't get nervous.

Rolling her shoulders, she pasted on a smile. She wasn't having the best morning to produce a real one, but she'd at least make it appear as if nothing was wrong in her life.

Absolutely nothing wrong.

Emma stopped in front of the counter and eyed the

pretty blonde talking a mile a minute on the phone. The blonde, whose hair looked perfectly combed into a ponytail that she knew she'd never be able to replicate, held up a finger to her with a friendly smile.

She smiled back, feeling obligated to do so, then carefully took her cream-colored knit hat off her head. She tried not to groan as she felt her hair stand straight up as if someone had rubbed a plastic balloon over her head to make her hair as staticky as they could. *I hate hats.* She rolled her eyes at her own thoughts. *No, you don't. You hate how perfect she looks.*

Trying to tame her dull brown hair as unobtrusively as she could, she waited impatiently for the woman to get off the dumb phone.

She wanted to get this over with and get out of town.

Fix her car.

Find a place to live.

Just...feel happy for once.

The woman ended the call, then gently laid the phone down on the cradle. Her ponytail bounced merrily as she shuffled a few things around her desk and then looked at Emma with a bright smile.

God, she hated that smile for some reason. Why did this woman have to look so joyous and happy?

"How can I help you?" That annoying smile was still plastered on her face.

Emma forced herself to keep the fake happiness displayed and resisted the temptation to fix her hair again. Her bland, almost mousy brown hair looked nothing like the perfection that was before her. It never would. She could never style it the way she liked. It lay past her shoulders, and with a lack of a haircut in over six months, one would probably be able to see the split ends if they looked closely enough. She didn't have time for a haircut with everything that had happened lately. Not that a haircut would have her looking as beautiful as this woman.

"Ma'am?"

Blinking, she realized she never responded. "Uh, yeah. I'm here to see Elliot Duncan."

A slow brow rose, yet with the same friendly smile in place. "Chief Duncan. Do you have an appointment?"

Chief Duncan. Well, excuse me. She almost blurted out that sarcastic comment.

"I don't. Is that a problem?"

The irritating woman shook her head, her annoying perfect blonde hair swinging with delight. "Of course not. I'll see if he's available." Her hand reached for the phone. "Can I have your name, please?"

She swallowed. "Emma." She fisted her hands. "Emma Brookes."

"Thank you." The woman punched a bunch of numbers and then started speaking.

Emma drifted away from the counter, suddenly wanting to flee fast and hard. What was she doing here? Why did she care so much?

"He'll be right here."

Emma looked at her, unable to hide the panic in her eyes.

"Are you okay?"

She nodded, then turned to get the hell out of this town. She changed her mind. She couldn't do this.

Hitting what felt like a brick wall, she almost fell before a strong arm grabbed her around the waist. The strong yet gentle touch immediately disappeared. For the tiniest of moments, she missed the touch, the strange tingling sensation that had zapped her when the man's fingers wrapped around her waist.

"I'm so sorry."

Her eyes drifted upward and met with a pair of startling hazel eyes, almost shimmering like golden tinsel hanging on a tree. Blinking, she tried to dislodge that silly notion. Golden tinsel? Ridiculous.

The man with the sparkling eyes she couldn't seem to tear her gaze from burrowed his brows in concern. "Did I hurt you?"

"I'm fine." She stepped back and to the side so he could pass.

He hesitated, then nodded and produced the biggest grin as he made eye contact with the beautiful woman behind the counter. Emma wanted to throw up. Why didn't he smile at her like that? Nobody ever smiled at her as if she were the most precious gem in the world.

Jealousy was a rabid disease. It did nothing but tear a person apart and turn them into someone with a black heart. She had no use for such emotion.

But eyeing this man, who she didn't know, as he looked at this woman, who she also didn't know, with such love and adoration made the jealousy coat every inch of her body. She wanted to shout at his back, "Look at me like that!"

"Bentley, are you okay? You gave us all a fright yesterday."

His grin widened, if that was even possible. "Perfectly fine. How are you, Daphne? Have you taken a breather at all today?"

"I just got off the phone with Theresa. We've been sharing the duty of gathering supplies."

"Well, that doesn't surprise me..."

Emma let their conversation drift away, closing her mind

off everything but her task. The same task she had been about to flee from. Nobody had ever accused her of being a coward, and they wouldn't start today.

Bentley.

Daphne.

What kind of names were those?

They were probably a couple. An annoying, sweet, sickening couple. A couple who probably did public displays of affection constantly, murmured *I love you* all the time. She had the urge to throw up again.

He looked just as perfect as the woman. His light brown hair was combed flawlessly. Although it was rather short, there wasn't much to style in any certain way. But still, pretty much picture perfect. And his smile was—

"Emma?"

Her head jerked to the right to a man she hadn't seen in ages. Fifteen years, to be exact.

"Is that really you?"

A small smile came out of nowhere. A real, genuine smile as the man she had looked up to for the brief time she knew him beamed at her brightly.

"It's me. I didn't know if you'd remember me or..."

Elliot grinned and held out his arms for a hug. She didn't hesitate. She stepped into his embrace and hugged him back, soaked up his affection and his warmth as much as she could. She'd need it for remembrance when she was alone, with nobody to cling to, to talk to. Just be with.

Elliot pulled her away, the same wonderful expression on his face. "It's been way too long. How's your father?" His smile dimmed a bit. "It's shameful to say, I haven't spoken to him in a few years."

Just like that, her feet ached to flee once again. She wanted to run out the door, get into her car that probably wouldn't start, and drive out of this town without a backward glance.

"Emma?" His thumb brushed a stray tear off her cheek.

She hadn't shed a tear in the longest time. She didn't even cry at the funeral. Why now? Why in front of him?

"He's dead." She said it without emotion.

She honestly had none left. No happiness. No joy. No worries.

The only emotion she could muster every minute, every second, of every day, was fear.

"I'm sorry to hear that." The expression on Elliot's face spoke the truth. She was sorry, too, but probably for a different reason. A tender arm wrapped around her shoulder. "Let's go to my office."

She nodded, her gaze drifting to the perfect couple behind them. She connected with Bentley's golden eyes, his annoying concern back in his glittering depths.

She didn't want his concern.

She didn't want anything—from anyone.

She wanted to do what she came here to do. Then leave.

Leave and hopefully find where she belonged in the world.

EMMA SAT down in front of Elliot's desk and threw out a grin for his sake when he held out a container full of cookies.

"My wife, Lynn, loves to bake. Her sugar cookies are the best."

Not wanting to appear rude, even though her nerves said she shouldn't take one bite, she grabbed a cookie shaped like Santa and took a small nibble. Delicious flavors hit her taste buds in all directions. A small moan might've even slipped out as she took another bite. Well, maybe her nerves weren't so bad where she couldn't enjoy this cookie.

"They're hard to resist." Elliot chuckled, as if he knew she didn't want the cookie to begin with, but thought it would make her feel better. Oddly enough, it did.

His smile gradually disappeared.

She knew what was coming. The awkwardness. The pity. The assumption that he understood what she was going through.

All of those things were her fault because she chose to come.

"How long ago did your father pass away?"

She took another bite of the cookie before responding. She knew this part of the questioning would occur, but she detested it. Every single part. "About six months ago. It was a heart attack. He didn't suffer." *I should know. I was there when it happened.*

His eyes crinkled with concern. "I'm sorry to hear that. He was a good man."

"Yeah, he loved retelling stories all the time. Shenanigans with you were one of his favorites."

Elliot laughed, a boisterous laugh that was so contagious, she couldn't help but join along. For the briefest of moments, she felt happy. Almost carefree. Like her life wasn't going to hell.

Then, he stopped. His eyes gathered more of that pity she hated seeing. The moment of happiness washed away as quickly as it appeared.

"I don't want to take much of your time. I was going through his stuff and I found some boxes..." A tiny breath escaped. "He wanted you to have some things. They're in my car."

More questions lingered in the depths of his eyes. Questions she didn't want to answer.

"I don't think he had anything of mine."

Shrugging, she took another bite of the cookie to prevent herself from blurting out something stupid—like the truth. Her dad had secrets she knew nothing about... until he died. Or how it took her five months to even go through his stuff. That it was forced upon her to do something because she couldn't keep up the payments on his house, and she had no money to store his belongings anywhere else. That she had no choice but to get rid of everything. That she was homeless and had nowhere to go.

"Are you okay, Emma? You..." He cleared his throat. "You should join us for supper tonight. I'd love for you to meet Lynn."

That sounded like the worst idea she'd ever heard.

And the best.

Saving money had always been difficult for her. Since her father passed away, forget it. She barely saw any green before it was taken from her hands immediately. For bills, for food, for gas. She had forty bucks in her purse, and that was it. Her bank account sat at zero. Her credit cards were maxed out.

She was broke.

Flat out broke.

"I think she mentioned something about making popcorn balls tonight with Laura. That's our daughter. It'll be fun."

She shouldn't.

But she wanted to so badly. She just didn't know how to say it.

She tore her gaze away from his kind, worried eyes, landing on the red stapler sitting near the edge of his desk.

Decorated with a colorful design on top with a winter scene, Santa and his eight reindeer flying through the sky with sprinkles of snow all around them, she couldn't stop the yearning for a wonderful Christmas this year. A yearning so strong, her heart started to ache with a deep, wrenching pain.

All because she eyed a dumb red stapler with a merry holiday theme painted on top.

It would never happen, though.

She didn't have money for a place to stay. How could she have a nice Christmas when she had no money?

"Emma?"

Her eyes jerked to his at the anguish in his tone. An understanding, unlike all those other times people gave her that look, hit her. He did understand. He knew the pain she was dealing with.

"Okay. Sure."

"Excellent. Lynn will be very excited to meet you."

Would she? This mysterious woman that seemed to have captured the heart of Elliot, a man she always looked up to as a father figure, would she want to meet her? She wasn't anybody special.

"Hey, Bentley. Come on in." Elliot's eyes darted behind her as a grin broke free, erasing the sorrow she saw moments before.

Turning slowly in her chair, she connected eyes with the man she didn't want to see again. She saw enough of his sickeningly sweet relationship to last her a lifetime.

"I didn't mean to intrude, Chief. Daphne said you had some boxes that I could take to the Daughtry family." His eyes wouldn't leave hers even as he spoke to Elliot. Her hands started to shake as her heart felt like it was pounding right out of her chest.

"I do." Elliot stood up and rounded his desk, then stopped near her. "This is Emma. A good friend of mine. Emma, this is Bentley. He works for the fire department."

Emma stood up, even though she wanted to ignore the guy, and gave him a tight nod that indicated she didn't care. Because she didn't. "Hi."

"It's nice to meet you."

"Are you busy, Emma? We could use the help." She looked at Elliot as he nodded toward Bentley. "He's bringing a load of supplies to the Daughtry family. They lost their house last night from a fire."

She shifted her gaze from Elliot back to Bentley. "Is your girlfriend helping, too?"

Bentley took a step backward as if in shock. And why wouldn't he? What kind of question was that? Hello, foot. Insert in mouth. Something she excelled at a little too often.

"I don't have a girlfriend." The surprise slid away as a silky grin touched his features. "Are you applying for the position?"

2

The audacity of this woman. Clearly, she didn't like him for some unknown reason, and then she asks him about his girlfriend as if she'd stepped into a pile of manure and the disgusting stench wouldn't disappear.

He didn't have a girlfriend.

Why would she care, anyway?

So he couldn't help but mess with her.

He needed the distraction. A lot.

Talking to Daphne moments before was hitting him like a Mack truck going eighty right into a brick building.

Yeah, he had no girlfriend. But he wanted one. Even though he teased with her to be his girlfriend, she wasn't the typical kind of woman he dated. He liked friendlier, light-hearted, sweet women.

Not the brash, brazen, and in-your-face kind of woman.

"Definitely not." She cocked a brow, as if waiting for some sort of witty retort from him.

He was honestly speechless. She said it as if revolted by the idea of dating him. What was wrong with him?

Nothing.

He held doors open. He made sure to walk his dates to the front door before leaving, and maybe even snatched a goodbye kiss, like a gentleman, of course. He paid for the meals, even sometimes surprising his date with a picnic in the park or in the woods on his parents' property. Hell, he even helped his buddy Aiden last year with a romantic gesture.

He knew how to treat a woman right. He was the utmost gentleman. Any woman would be lucky to have him as a boyfriend.

Except Daphne. She obviously didn't think he was that great. She was marrying someone else.

Maybe there was something wrong with him.

"I was joking around. It's nice to meet you, Emma." He cleared his throat and tossed a look at Chief Duncan, who looked entirely too amused by the odd exchange. "I can handle this on my own, Chief. If you direct me to where the boxes are at, I'll take care of it."

The chief hesitated, but then smiled as he nodded. "There are five boxes in the break room filled with clothes. I'll be heading over to the farm later today with some food that Lynn's preparing. Thanks, Bentley."

"Of course. Give me a call if you need any other help." He gave Emma a brisk nod and walked out of the office before he said something that would completely embarrass him.

Well, fine. He might not be on the top of his game at the moment when it came to women, but did she have to sound so appalled by the idea of dating him? What was her problem, anyway? She acted weird from the moment he accidentally ran into her.

Maybe that's why she had a bug up her ass. She didn't appreciate him getting in her way.

Well, sorry. He had a lot on his mind. From the fire that took everything from a good family. To the disastrous countdown to Daphne's wedding.

Life sucked.

"Hey, man. Just starting your shift?"

Aiden nodded as he shut the fridge in the break room. "Yep. How's it going? You okay? Theresa's been worried about you."

"Fit as a fiddle. I wasn't in that much danger." Sort of a lie. But Aiden didn't need to know how close he came to being in some serious trouble.

He had yet to meet with the fire chief. When he wanted, he could procrastinate like the best of them.

A stern expression etched across Aiden's face as his eyes narrowed. "That's not what I heard."

Shrugging, not in the mood to hash it over, he grabbed a box. "I have to get these to the Daughtry's. Grab one and let's walk."

Aiden's eyes narrowed even more before he decided to drop the subject and grabbed a box. They headed for the front entrance where he parked his truck.

"Did you meet Emma? She's weird as shit."

"I have not had the pleasure. Who is she, and why do you think she's weird?" Aiden chuckled as if he knew something Bentley didn't.

"She's some friend of Chief Duncan's. And she's...she's weird. Trust me on this one."

"Yeah, like the time I trusted you to get us home from the Cities when my car broke down and we ended up sleeping in a rat-infested motel instead of our comfy beds."

A deep laugh rang in the hallway. "A fluke in my abilities. Nothing more. I know what I'm talking about here."

"This is good." Aiden smiled wide as he winked at Daphne before pushing the door open with his shoulder and stepped outside. "This is really good."

Bentley stopped on the sidewalk, the cold wind biting his cheeks, as he watched Aiden set the box on the bed of the truck. "What are you talking about? What is good?" Even though he liked seeing his best friend back to himself —smiling, winking, actually looking happy—he didn't like the tone of his voice. So devious.

His smile grew. "This Emma chick."

"There's nothing good about her. Nothing." Bentley tossed his box right next to Aiden's.

"Oh, this is better than I thought."

His brows puckered. "Stop talking in riddles. I just told you she was weird."

Aiden slapped him on the shoulder as he laughed way harder than he should've. "Maybe. But she's the first woman you've said one word about...besides Daphne. This is good. I like Emma. I should go introduce myself."

Aiden walked away and opened the door.

"You're heading for the break room to grab another box, right?"

"Of course not. I'm going to meet Emma." Aiden's laughter rang around his head as the door closed behind him.

What just happened?

Did his best friend just mess with him? About a woman?

While he liked hearing his friend laughing and enjoying life again, he didn't appreciate that it was directed at him. Not cool.

He dated here and there. He didn't pine over Daphne

like a pathetic little schoolboy. At least, not in front of others. When he was alone, the loneliness, the quietness surrounding him, he might brood a little bit more than was proper.

When he officially decided it was time to find the woman he wanted to marry, it certainly wouldn't be some sassy, annoying woman that thought dating him was repulsive.

Deciding he would ignore Aiden, he walked back inside without looking at Daphne, something he rarely did when she was near, and grabbed the remaining three boxes as fast as he could. He didn't run into Aiden, Emma, or Chief Duncan while he finished the task. Thankfully.

He dropped the boxes off to the Daughtry's farm where they were staying in the barn. They were fortunate enough they had a heating system in the barn. Joe Daughtry, the father, had an office that was big enough for them to sleep in until they could find another place to live temporarily while they rebuilt. They needed to be on the farm for the animals.

The town had already started to rally together, providing the family with cots to sleep on, blankets, pillows, clothes, food, and anything else they would need immediately.

Bentley didn't mind transporting all the goods either.

As soon as he finished chit-chatting with the Daughtry's, he knew he had stalled long enough. Time to face the fire chief and see how much trouble he was in.

Yeah, he ran back into a burning building after orders not to do so.

He'd do it all over again.

Because the smile on the little girl's face as she hugged her puppy tight was worth every torturous second he endured inside that house.

EMMA HUNG BACK EVEN though Elliot held out his arm for her to step closer as he introduced her to Lynn, his wife. She seemed like a nice lady. Beautiful with a friendly smile that had no malice behind the depths. And extremely pregnant, as she waddled closer to shake her hand. Hell, Emma knew she was going to meet her considering Elliot walked her across the street from the precinct to the bakery to do just that.

"It's so nice to meet you, Emma. Elliot's said such wonderful things about you."

"Really?"

She couldn't hold back the surprise. She hadn't seen Elliot in over fifteen years. He talked about her? She was that rememberable?

She found the idea rather preposterous.

Lynn offered her another sweet smile. "Of course. Your father was an important part of his life. He said you were full of life, laughter, and so much fun. You loved to play pranks." She leaned closer. "He's gotten me good a few times too many. I think I need some help from an expert."

Emma couldn't help it. A tiny smile filtered out as ideas flooded her mind. She loved to play pranks when she was younger. She hadn't done anything like that in the longest time. She barely remembered what it was like to have fun.

"She's an expert, Lynn. Just a fair warning." They both turned to Elliot, who had a silly grin on his face.

"Good. Watch your back, sweetheart." Lynn turned her attention Emma's way and winked as if they were now best friends and would be playing a great joke on Elliot. "Would you like something to eat?"

"I'm good. I already had one of your cookies. Delicious. Thank you."

"I invited Emma over tonight for supper. Do you have plans for the rest of the day, Emma?" Elliot asked, a sprinkle of concern hidden in his gaze.

He was trying to hide it from her, but she saw it. And she didn't want it. She didn't need anyone's concern. Or help.

But she couldn't confess she had no plans. No money. Nowhere to go.

"Not really." That answer would have to suffice.

"That's perfect. Would you mind helping Lynn out today? Stacey, who normally helps her, called out sick. A nasty bug has been floating around town." Elliot's eyes crinkled with worry as they hit Lynn. "A bug I hope stays away from here."

Lynn looked back at him with love, but didn't say anything. It's as if they communicated their worries with each other without saying one word. Elliot saying how much he loved her and didn't want her to get sick. And Lynn reassuring him she would be fine and he shouldn't worry so much.

Emma stood there with awe. What would it be like to have the kind of relationship where you could communicate without speaking?

She'd probably never know.

"I would appreciate the help, Emma. If you don't mind."

Lynn's soft voice helped her decide pretty quickly. "Sure. I'd love to help." How could she say no to that?

She had nothing better to do, anyway, other than stress about where she'd be spending the night. Even staying in her car, something she wasn't unfamiliar with, wouldn't work tonight or for the rest of the winter. She'd freeze to death.

"Great. Why don't you grab the apron hanging on the hook over there and start packing those cookies for me." Lynn pointed to the containers and pans of cookies sitting on a table near her. It all looked easy enough. "There's gloves on the table near the door. I need to go back out front. It's been busy today."

"I'll be back later. Have fun, Emma." Elliot gave her a sweet smile as he walked out of the swinging doors with Lynn leading the way.

She grabbed the apron hanging on a peg near the doors and then grabbed some gloves. As she started to package the cookies, ten cookies per package, a silly smile touched her face.

What a strange day.

She would've never guessed when she drove into town she'd be working in a bakery, looking forward to supper tonight with two great people. She didn't know Lynn as she did Elliot, but she already liked her. A lot.

It'd be hard to leave.

Without warning, another annoying person entered her thoughts.

Bentley.

Ugh. She wouldn't miss that irritating man.

Nope.

Not one bit.

"YOU SHOULD GO."

Elliot nuzzled her neck as his hands slid around her waist and rested on her plump belly. "I'm worried about you. Don't work too hard. Let Emma do any heavy lifting. I'm sure she won't mind."

"I'll be fine."

A kiss touched her neck. "You're seven months pregnant, and I can worry if I want to."

Lynn turned around in his arms and grabbed a quick kiss, then looked over his shoulder at Mrs. Newton. "I'll be right with you. You're going to love the design on the cake."

"Oh, I'm sure I will, Lynn. I always love your creativity. Don't mind me. You can give the chief one more kiss," Mrs. Newton said with a chuckle as her gaze went back to the display case in front of her.

Elliot laughed as his hands tightened around her waist. "I wish I could do more than kiss you right now." His laughter died, as did his smile. "I'm worried about Emma. She was close with her dad. She's acting all nonchalant that he's gone, but I don't think she is. See if you can work your magic."

A tiny giggle escaped. "What magic is that?"

"I don't know. You have such a special way with Laura. Like when those girls were picking on her at school a few months ago and she didn't want to talk about it. You finally got her to talk."

"She's also my daughter. We have a close relationship." Concern touched her eyes. "But I know what you mean. I saw something in her eyes." Her gaze lowered. "I saw a little of me when I was close to that age."

Elliot lifted her chin with a touch of a finger. "See. That's the magic I'm talking about." He kissed her. "I'll be back later."

A tender smile appeared. "I look forward to it."

3

Emma stood to the side as Lynn remade the bed in the guest room of their home. The bed looked fine before Lynn started messing with it, but she decided it wasn't worth saying anything. The look Lynn had in her eyes said arguing wouldn't sway her from remaking the bed with fresh sheets.

"I'm so happy. Christmastime around here is so much fun. So magical. You'll love it."

Emma only offered a small grin. She wasn't so sure it would be fun and magical, but she already said she'd stay with them through the holidays.

How did it happen?

She still couldn't figure it out.

One minute she was talking to Lynn in the bakery, superficial stuff, barely even grazing the surface of the problems in her life. The next minute, Lynn was insisting she stay with them until after Christmas.

She barely hesitated saying yes. For the next two and a half weeks, she had a roof over her head, food in her belly, and money in her pockets. That was the biggest decision factor.

Lynn asked her to help in the bakery during the holidays, because it was the busiest time of year for her, and she would pay her. A decent amount, too. She definitely couldn't say no to that.

"There. Fresh sheets. I always love sleeping in fresh, clean sheets." Lynn stood back as she looked at her handy work with a bright smile. It almost made Emma want to smile. But she didn't.

"I appreciate everything you're doing for me."

"You're like family. Of course we want you here." Lynn placed a tender hand on her shoulder, then left the room.

Like family?

She didn't even know Lynn. She only knew Elliot, and it had been fifteen years since she last saw him.

A ten-year-old little girl, full of life and laughter and so many dreams. Every time she saw Elliot, her world seemed a little better, a little brighter.

He had been the uncle she never had.

Then he left.

It went right back to just her and her dad. Back to loneliness. Back to her dad always working and no one around to play with. Back to barely anyone caring about her.

After that, she never let anyone else in. She never let anyone have the chance at her heart. It was too painful when they left.

A knock sounded on the doorframe. "Can I come in?"

She turned toward the door and nodded at Elliot. "Thanks for letting me stay for a while."

A sincere smile graced his handsome face, two little dimples forming, reminding her of her dad. Like a knife to the heart. His smile fell. "I sense something is bothering you. You know I'm here if you need to talk about anything. I'm really glad you're staying. It'll be nice to catch up."

She didn't need him digging into her feelings, or worrying about her, so she pulled out a smile that she hoped would appease him, that would show she was perfectly fine. And she was. She would be. "I'd love to catch up. You have a beautiful home."

Her smile must've eased his worries because his frown disappeared. "Lynn's making popcorn balls with Laura. Do you want to come help?"

Her eyes bulged as laughter escaped her. Real laughter. "She spent all day baking. Why is she baking some more?"

"She loves to bake." He laughed, the sound almost filling up her heart. "It's also for Laura to take to school, so we can't eat them all."

Emma chuckled as she followed him out of the room. "And you would eat them all, wouldn't you?"

"You bet."

The light sound of Christmas music drifted their way as they walked to the kitchen. Emma couldn't hold back the smile as she saw Lynn and Laura mixing something at the stove, and Gregory, Elliot's dad, slathering his hands with butter. A large bowl of popcorn sat on the table next to a few sheets of wax paper.

Gregory beamed at her as soon as he saw her. "Come here, darling. You can help me form the balls. Now, there's a right way to make them. I'll show you how to do it properly."

"Grandpa, you can't screw up making these," Laura said sweetly.

"Ha! You can. Elliot always presses them too hard." Gregory grinned as he winked at Elliot, who laughed like he agreed. "I bet you I make the best looking popcorn balls tonight. Nice and soft, yet round. Winner gets to pick out the Christmas movie for tonight." Gregory then winked at Laura, as if they were sharing a secret joke.

"You're on. I'll be winning tonight." Emma interlocked her fingers and pulled them back as if cracking her knuckles, ready to win a fight. She might not know what joke they were sharing, but she'd play along.

Gregory graced her with a wily smile and pulled out a chair for her. "You're on, girlie. Prepare to lose."

Emma took a seat. For the first time in the longest time, she felt content. Almost happy.

BENTLEY TOOK a sip of beer as the stool next to him shifted and his best friend took a seat.

"Why aren't you at home with your beautiful wife?"

Aiden ordered a beer from Stu and grinned. "Because my best friend needs me." His grin dimmed. "Seriously, I was the master at hiding my feelings. What's going on? How you holding up?"

Bentley resisted rolling his eyes. "I'm fine. I didn't get a scratch in that house. I wish everyone would leave me alone about it."

"Not what I was talking about, but we can go there first. The fire chief reamed you out, huh?"

He took another sip of beer to stop the angry words that wanted to spill out. Not here. Not with an audience. Maybe if he was at home, just him and Aiden, he'd tell him how he felt about the things the fire chief said. But not here.

"That bad?"

"I'm not officially suspended, but I've been told to take a few days off." He muttered under his breath. "Not really off either. He wants me to donate my time getting the dumb Christmas party ready."

He wanted to hit Aiden in the face when he started laughing as if it was the funniest thing he'd ever heard. There was nothing funny about having to work on the annual Christmas party. Sure, he might've helped in the past, but this year...

This year Daphne wouldn't be there.

She'd be getting ready for her wedding in two and a half weeks.

Life just sucked.

And the worst pest in the world was already grating on his nerves.

Marybeth.

Bentley, I need you to do this. I need you to do that. I need you to bend over backwards to do my bidding.

Well, maybe she didn't say those exact words, but that's how he heard it. He was already going out of his mind, and he had only been in her presence for thirty minutes today.

"Sorry. That's not funny." Aiden continued to chuckle. "You know we won't be there this year."

"Why not?"

"Theresa's super busy with jewelry orders and...and she doesn't want to go. She says she doesn't fit in with that world." Aiden rolled his eyes. "I prefer not to argue with my wife, even though I don't agree with her. How is the decorating going? Last year wasn't so bad."

"Ha! You had Theresa there with you. And Marybeth can be such a bitch. I don't want to work with her."

"You don't have to tell me. I'm not surprised she's already getting on your nerves." Aiden couldn't hold back another chuckle as Bentley nodded in confirmation. "What you need is something to distract you. From everything."

He cocked his head to the side as he met Aiden's eyes. "Like what? What could possibly make dealing with Marybeth better and...yeah, all that other shit."

He didn't need to say Daphne's name to know that's what Aiden was referring to, what he wanted to talk about in the beginning when he sat down.

"I don't know. You could adopt a dog."

That garnered a chuckle. "You have the dumbest ideas sometimes. I live in a small house and I work too much to take care of a dog."

"Hey, at least I'm offering ideas. I won't let you sulk. Not like I did for far too long before I opened myself up to Theresa." Aiden sighed. "Are you sad Daphne is getting married because she was the one that got away? Or are you sad because now you can't use her as your crutch to avoid women? Did she really get away? Because, the way I remember it, you walked away without glancing back. Then suddenly, it's as if the world ended when she got a boyfriend."

He jerked at the words Aiden flung at him. As if he was attacking him for some unknown reason. What the hell? Why?

Aiden laid a hand on his shoulder. He immediately shook him off.

"I'm not trying to be an asshole, but, Bentley, think about it. I hate seeing you like this. I want to help."

He stood up abruptly, his stool almost toppling over. "By saying shit like that. That I was making excuses. That I never wanted her. That I was hiding behind something. How, Aiden? How is that helping?" He shook his head, holding in some unsavory words that wanted to fly out. "See you around."

He walked out of the bar and jumped into his truck

before Aiden could stop him. The drive home was quick, considering he only lived five minutes from the bar. He could've walked if he wanted to brave the cold for that long. He knew Theresa used to love to walk everywhere. She didn't own a car until she moved in with Aiden. He could never figure out how she could stand walking all the time in the blistering cold.

The cold air swept through him as he stepped out of the truck and stopped, listened, and pondered what the hell just happened with his best friend.

Maybe she walked every day in the cold to release some tension. Because, as he stood, letting the icy air seep into his veins, some of the tension from moments before left.

He eyed his front door for a half second before he turned around and started walking. And walking. Until he hit the park less than a minute from his house.

He didn't notice the lone figure on the swing until he was halfway across the park. Curiosity took over the rest of the way.

Without a word, he took the swing right next to the last person he wanted to talk to.

Emma.

4

"Who said you could join me?"

"Santa Claus. He said you're on the naughty list. I'm here to fix that."

Cocking a brow, Emma glared his way. "How so?"

"Well, we could start with the stick up your ass and go from there."

Despite how rude that sounded, she laughed, especially when she saw the twinkle in his eye when he said it. She also didn't miss the anguish mingled in the depths. He was hurting somehow. Not that it was any of her business. But he made it her business when he sat down next to her.

"It's up there kind of far. I don't think you can handle the task."

His eyes glittered in the dark. "I can handle anything you throw at me."

She chuckled. "We'll see. You look like a pansy. I have doubts."

A low rumble escaped his lips as he pushed his foot to the ground, swinging a little. His mouth kept twitching, as if he wanted to burst out laughing, but held himself back. For some odd reason, she wanted to hear him laugh. A real, true laugh. Maybe it would lift her spirits some.

Or maybe he intrigued her a little too much.

"Why are you out here?"

She decided to start a little swinging as well. "Why are you?"

"I needed some fresh air."

Her eyes connected with his, almost swinging in sync as they shared a mutual understanding of some sort. He didn't say much, but what he said was enough. She heard it in the way the words left his mouth, the way his eyes bled with pain.

She looked away.

She didn't know what to make of this guy. Why she sensed a camaraderie of sorts. She didn't want to connect with anyone here. She didn't want to like anyone she met.

A slow breath released.

Too late.

She already adored Laura, who had the sweetest laugh. She admired Lynn, an ambitious, loving woman. She envied Elliot, who had a wonderful family he'd do anything and everything for. She loved how Gregory already insisted she call him grandpa, as if she were part of the family.

She liked them all. Which would make it that much harder when she had to leave.

Now she was starting to like this irritating man, who had yet to say anything nice. More like tease her mercilessly, and he didn't even know her enough to act that way.

They swung in silence. Surprisingly, he didn't press her further after he shared his reason for being out here. She was beyond grateful for that small reprieve. She didn't want to tell him, or anyone, why she slipped out of Elliot's house, through a window no less, to have a moment to herself.

She retired to her bedroom, claiming she was tired, and then snuck out the window as if she were a teenager sneaking out for a night of fun.

She needed some fresh air.

Like he said.

"So, what's your deal with blondie?"

"Who?"

Glancing at him, she didn't miss the flash of awareness even though he feigned confusion. "The blonde chick you couldn't keep your eyes off of. The one you were drooling over. Her. Don't act all dumb."

He snickered. "Because you know me so well to know how I'm acting."

"I can read people well. My dad was in law enforcement my entire life. He taught me how to pick out a suspect, how to note anything strange, how to protect myself, how to shoot a weapon...how to know when someone's lying."

A low sigh rented the air as he looked away. "Her name is Daphne and she's a friend. Nothing more."

"Wow. You're a terrible liar." She rolled her eyes. "Try again."

A soft laugh swirled around them. "She is my friend." His foot dug into the ground a little harder than was necessary as he continued to push himself in a slow swinging motion.

"But you want more?"

He shrugged. "It doesn't matter what I want, she's getting married on Christmas Eve."

A full bout of laughter fell out of her. "That's the dumbest thing I ever heard."

At first, he looked pissed. Beyond pissed. For the briefest

of moments, she regretted laughing as hard as she did. His fierce look even made her slightly nervous. She didn't know him that well. Was he a violent man?

Then, like a storm that came out of nowhere, ending just as abruptly, the sun coming in as if not a drop of rain occurred, he smiled. "What's so dumb? That I'm still pining over her?"

"No. Getting married near Christmas." She shrugged. "I don't know who picked the date, but if she did, she wasn't thinking clearly."

"How so?"

Meeting his gaze, she smiled devilishly. "Now she'll only get one set of presents for Christmas and her anniversary. Kind of like people who have a birthday near Christmas. I'm sure it's all rolled into one. Boring." She made sure to emphasize how boring that would be.

His brows puckered as if contemplating what she said really hard. "That's a good point. I think she did pick the date. She loves Christmas."

"So? I like Christmas, but I'd never want to get married around it."

"Because you wouldn't get as many presents. Conceited much?"

Sticking out her tongue at him, she laughed. "Maybe."

Or maybe she never had a relationship where a guy showered her with gifts, or even with something as simple as his love. When she finally did get that special someone in her life, she didn't want to share it with a huge holiday like Christmas.

"I dated her in high school, about four months."

Jerking her attention at him, she almost felt sorry for him. The way his head hung low, the sadness surrounding him like his dog died or something.

"Seriously?" She laughed again. A loud, boisterous laugh that almost made her stomach hurt. She couldn't remember the last time she laughed this much. But, boy, it felt...good.

"Why do you insist on laughing at everything I say?"

"You're just a funny guy. It's really easy." A few more snickers escaped. "Four months? In high school? How old are you? Dude, come on."

"Dude?" This time he rolled his eyes. "I'm twenty-six, thank you. Yeah, it might've been a silly high school romance, but I didn't realize at the time how special she was. By the time I did, she was with another guy. So I let the good one get away."

She covered her mouth with her hand as she tried to keep the laughter in. It didn't work.

"Go ahead, laugh. Not sure why it's so funny."

"Excuses much?" She let her hand drop as her laughter circled them. "Come on. She can't be that special. Remember, she's getting married near Christmas. That's a huge point against her."

"Whatever. Moving on. Now you tell me something so I can laugh at you." He gestured his hand in a circle for her to start sharing.

"I can burp the alphabet." She couldn't stop the large smile that spread across her face as he busted out laughing.

"I'll take your word for it."

"Are you sure? I'd be more than happy to demonstrate."

"I insist. Hold it in."

They both laughed a little more, then silence descended. A weird, almost comfortable silence. She never shared this sort of closeness with anyone.

Well, she used to with her best friend. But Ashley...

She abruptly stood up. "I should go."

He looked surprised, but nodded. "I'll walk—"

"Don't." She held her hand up and shook her head. "Don't act like a gentleman. I prefer to think of you as an annoying nuisance."

He grinned. "As you wish, my lady."

Rolling her eyes, she chuckled. "You're so weird."

She turned around and started walking away.

"Hey...Emma."

His soft voice as he said her name slid down her spine with a feeling she had never felt before. She didn't turn around to face him for that reason alone, but she did stop walking.

"I'm helping to decorate for the annual Christmas party coming up. I don't know how long you'll be in town, but..." His voice trailed off.

She almost started walking again, yet she stood immobile, waiting, almost fearing what he might say.

"It's the most boring thing ever. And dealing with...some people can try anyone's patience. Do you want to help me?"

Did she?

Did she want to forge more friendships just to have them all ripped away from her when she left?

No.

No, she didn't.

She continued walking without one word in response.

BENTLEY BLEW OUT A SLOW BREATH, grateful, so very grateful, it was Donna Contreas, the organizer for the annual Christmas party, heading his way and not Marybeth.

"Bentley, it's so kind of you to help us out. The Christmas party is tomorrow, and I feel like I'm pulling my hair out. We have help coming tonight to set up most of the decorations, but I need you to grab the tables and chairs from Bernie before everyone gets here."

"No problem, Mrs. Contreas. It shouldn't take me too long."

The smile she beamed at him was enough to make him feel slightly better for being forced to help. He didn't mind helping. Honestly, he didn't. He just didn't want it getting around that he was *forced* to help. A dumb unofficial suspension for saving a puppy's life.

So far, everyone still considered him a hero.

He couldn't dispute that. It was idiotic and careless to run back into that building, but no matter how long he lay awake and ran the events over and over in his mind, he couldn't find another alternative. He still would've gone back into the house to save the dog.

And thinking about the fire had been better than thinking about Emma.

Beautiful, aggravating Emma.

That woman could skewer a man with one simple look. She already did multiple times with him. And her words. Sassy and sharp.

He didn't like women like that. He liked them sweet and docile. Like Daphne.

So why did his mind keep conjuring Emma?

He barely slept a wink last night thinking and analyzing everything that was said between them.

Or the fact she never answered his question. His stupid, idiotic question.

He still couldn't figure out what had possessed him to ask her to help. He barely liked her, so why would he want her around him even more?

Even his reasoning had been lame. Dealing with her over Marybeth would be ten times better. It honestly would.

It was still a lame reason to ask her to help him.

It didn't matter. Her silence had been answer enough.

He left the hotel where the annual Christmas party was held every year and headed down the street to Bernie's Hardware Store. He spoke with Bernie about the tables and chairs, then headed outside to pull his truck to the back of the store. Bernie had a huge storage area in the back where he held supplies of all kinds for people to rent.

His steps slowed as he came upon Lynn's bakery, Sweet Treats Delight, and saw Emma behind the counter. She looked happy and cute dressed in a white apron with what appeared to be something purple streaked across the front, and her golden brown hair pulled into a ponytail. Although a few strands fell out, framing her face and enhancing her beauty somehow. Normally, hair was hair. Up, down, short, long. He didn't care how a woman styled it. But right now, Emma's hair made her look more exquisite than the last time he saw her. The simplicity of how she wore it. Not even caring it wasn't pulled back with perfection.

Like Daphne always wore her hair. Not a strand ever out of place.

Seriously. Why was he comparing them? There was no comparison. Daphne was...what? Better than Emma? No, he couldn't say that. But he could admit Emma was way different than Daphne, and he...liked that. He couldn't even explain to himself the reason why.

Before he could stop himself, he pulled open the door and entered the bakery. Well, he didn't eat breakfast. That excuse was as good as any.

Their eyes connected.

She smiled at Debbie, a good friend of Lynn's who lived

a town over in Mason, and then frowned as he approached the counter.

Oddly enough, that frown made him smile. He secretly loved how she got annoyed with him simply by seeing his face. It was also a mystery why he felt that way.

Debbie greeted him with a friendly hello, which he returned in kind, then she left. He approached the counter, undeterred by Emma's scary glare.

"What do you want?" Her brows puckered low as her frown turned almost vicious.

A silky grin emerged. "What does anybody want when they come into a bakery? Something sweet."

She rolled her eyes. "Was that some kind of cheesy pickup line? Because it was seriously lame."

He laughed. "Emma sweetheart, if I was trying to use a pickup line on you, you'd blush and stutter all over your words."

Her beautiful laughter rang throughout, filling his heart with a giddy joy he wasn't used to feeling. His mind started conjuring more ways to get her to laugh like that.

"You're impossible. I have never blushed or stuttered over a man in my life, and I'm not going to start now."

Leaning gently against the counter, he grinned. "Challenge accepted."

Rolling her eyes again, she plucked a wax tissue paper out of the box sitting on the counter and grabbed a chocolate covered doughnut with red and green sprinkles from the display case, and set it in front of him. "There. Now go away."

"I didn't order a doughnut."

"I don't care. Take it and leave. You're annoying me."

"Are you buying me a doughnut? Is this, like, an unofficial first date?" He couldn't hold back a grin as her eyes narrowed.

"Consider it a bribe to leave me the hell alone."

He grabbed the doughnut, because it did look delicious and he was hungry, and smiled wider. "I'll pick you up at five."

"Excuse me?"

"To help decorate for the Christmas party."

"I never said I'd help."

"You also never said no." He couldn't help but flash her his signature grin that usually had women melting at his feet. He also tossed a five on the counter, not willing to let her pay for his doughnut when he had every intention of purchasing something anyway, and then turned around to leave.

"Forget it. I'm not helping you. You don't even know where I'm staying."

"It's a small town. I can figure it out." He waved goodbye and stepped outside, the door closing behind him and Emma's sweet anger drifting away. He bit into the doughnut and sighed happily.

Lynn sure knew how to bake. He didn't care what he ordered or what he ate of hers, it always tasted delicious.

By the time he walked to his truck, he had inhaled the doughnut and tossed the waxed tissue paper on the floor of the passenger side.

It didn't take long to load up the tables and chairs and deliver them to the hotel. Although it did take him quite a few trips to deliver the amount of tables and chairs Donna wanted for the party. Most of the town, at least the ones lucky enough to be invited, showed up.

Their town might pull together in a crisis, but at times, they showed how conceited and stuck up they could be.

Bentley understood Theresa's reasoning for not wanting to go to the Christmas party. Most of the people invited were from the city council, and their family and friends, and anyone else considered important. Since most of the businesses on Main Street helped supply the party, of course they received an invitation, like Bernie. Although, come to think of it, Bernie never showed up.

Bentley couldn't blame him. It was a stuffy event, besides the part where everyone brought a present to put under the big tree that sat in the middle of the ballroom.

That was his favorite part. The day after the party, sometimes a few days after, the fire department would round up all the presents and deliver them to the children and local shelters around the area in the fire truck. He always loved seeing the excited gleam in the children's eyes as they pulled up to the hospital entrance with gifts galore.

The nurses would bring the kids capable enough to pick out a present, and if they were able to, take a look inside the truck. The other presents they would deliver room to room. Even though some were confined to a bed, they still had that excited gleam in their eye when they entered the room with a Santa bag filled with goodies.

When he finished unloading all the tables and chairs, also completing a few other minor tasks for Donna, Bentley realized he barely had enough time to head home for a quick bite to eat and a shower.

He didn't need to take a shower, considering he'd be doing more heavy labor putting up decorations, but he wanted to look refreshed for Emma.

Strange.

It had been a long time, a very long time, since he actually wanted to impress a woman.

Emma would be the hardest woman he'd ever had to impress.

Why was he trying so hard with her? She didn't like him. He didn't even like her.

As he stepped out of the shower, the steam swirling around, the heat soothing, he realized he was lying to himself.

He did like her.

He liked her a lot.

He liked her honesty. Her smile. The mischievous intent that twinkled in her eyes.

She was no Daphne.

He almost tripped putting on his pants as that thought rolled through his mind.

She definitely was no Daphne.

Damn if he didn't like her even more for that reason.

Well, shit.

Maybe Aiden hit it on the mark. Maybe he had pined and wallowed a little too hard over a woman who probably would've never lasted longer than a few months.

Because, as he shoved on his shirt, it occurred to him that Daphne never made his heart race, made his nerves go haywire, or made his mind run in overdrive trying to come up with something witty and cute to say.

Emma did.

Emma challenged him. She made him work for her attention, for her sweet smiles and beautiful laugh.

That's what he liked in a woman.

Not sweet and docile. Not like Daphne.

Shaving quickly, although carefully, he couldn't stop the strange giddiness that pounded in his heart.

He was nervous.

Extremely nervous.

He had no idea if something between them was possible, but for the first time in the longest time, he was willing to find out.

He was done hiding behind his silly crush on Daphne.

He was done making excuses of why his dates and short-term girlfriends never worked out.

He liked Emma.

It was time to put the full-on Bentley charm to work.

5

Emma glanced at the clock hanging above the television for the umpteenth time.

Damn the man!

He was actually making her anticipate his arrival. No man had ever done that before. Usually, when getting ready for a date—not that she considered this a date—she was at least twenty minutes behind on getting ready when they picked her up. They would be forced to wait for her in the living room as she finished applying her makeup and doing her hair that never turned out the way she wanted it to.

Now, here's Bentley, a man who didn't even know where she was staying, although claiming he could figure it out, making her constantly check the clock every other minute until it hit five.

She had three minutes to go.

Not that she considered this a date, because she totally didn't. Since this absolutely was not a date, she already had her makeup and hair done because she decided not to do a damn thing. She still looked sweaty and tired from working all day in the bakery. Her hair was a mess, sitting in a ponytail with a few strands hanging out. Her mascara was still holding strong, but her eye shadow had started to fade, considering she started to rub her eyes a few times, then stopped when she realized she wore makeup. She didn't even reapply any lipstick.

He wanted her to help put up some dumb decorations, then this was how he was going to get her. Looking like a straggly monster after a hard day's work.

Jerking in surprise, it occurred to her—why was she even considering going with him if he showed up? She should slam the door in his face. She never agreed to this. She didn't have to help him do a damn thing.

The clock on the wall hit five o'clock.

For a moment, she expected gongs to ring out throughout the house.

The only noises she heard were Lynn and Laura making sounds from the kitchen as they prepared supper together. Gregory, as she was told, was out with his girlfriend Gabby for the night. Elliot was outside shoveling the porch from the light dusting of snow that started about two hours ago.

"Hey, Emma, you have a visitor."

She jerked her head to the hallway where Elliot stood next to Bentley with a dose of concern etched on his face, as if he were her father and didn't know why Bentley was here.

And Bentley. Her breath caught in her throat at the sight of him. He looked like he had changed and cleaned himself up. For her? But why? His jaw looked smooth to the touch. She almost wanted to stand up, walk over to him, and run a hand across his jaw to find out how smooth it was. His eyes twinkled at her with mischief and delight. As if he knew what she was thinking.

A spark of desire settled in her stomach at the sight.

Maybe, just maybe, she had been anticipating his arrival a little more than she wanted to admit.

"Are you ready?"

Bentley's question went deeper than she imagined. Was she ready? She wasn't sure she was prepared for anything. Not a damn thing. Especially the way he was making her feel.

She stood up abruptly. "I never said I would be helping you. Go to hell, Bentley."

She didn't miss the flash of surprise in Elliot's eyes as she stormed out of the living room and went to her room, where she slammed her door for good measure as if she were a bratty teenager acting out. And honestly, she wasn't blind to the fact she *was* acting bratty. Downright ridiculous.

Sitting down on the edge of the bed, she closed her eyes and tried to pretend she didn't act like a complete baby.

What was the big deal if she went with him to hang stupid decorations?

The door opened and closed softly. A weight shifted the bed as someone sat next to her. Most likely Elliot to find out why she was acting like a petulant child.

A warm hand curled around hers that she was squeezing tightly together. The touch sent a zap of warm desire straight to her core. Her eyes popped open. Turning her head, her gaze met Bentley's.

"I've been to hell before. Two days ago. Fire burning all around me. I thought for a moment I was going to die." He released a slow breath. His head twitched as if he wanted to look away, but he didn't. "My boss didn't officially suspend me, but he told me to take a few days off and help with the Christmas party. My penance for acting like an idiot. So, yeah, I've been to hell. I don't want to go back."

His fingers were tight against hers. She could feel the

strength in his small touch, but also his anguish that she had heard in each word.

"It's nothing exciting hanging decorations, but I find myself enjoying your company. So I thought it'd be nice if you came with. If you don't want to, I'm not going to make you." His eyes sparkled as his head moved closer, almost as if he wanted to kiss her. Then he stopped moving altogether.

She had no idea what to say. She only wanted him to keep inching closer until his mouth touched hers.

"I won't bother you again." He stood up and headed for the door.

"I haven't eaten yet. I get cranky when I'm hungry." That was her reasoning for being a bitch and she wouldn't be saying otherwise. He could take it or leave it.

He swiveled toward her and grinned. "I know the perfect place to swing by and get a burger."

"As long as they don't put ketchup on it. I hate ketchup." She stood up slowly, unsure why she was changing her mind and going with him. Letting this man in her heart, even a little bit, would break her. It would tear her apart when she left. It always did when she lost someone she cared about.

The barrier around her heart thickened. The wall, tall and strong, she fortified as a child, got taller. She'd help Bentley with these dumb decorations, but she wouldn't allow him to penetrate any of her defenses. She could do this. No problem.

"No ketchup. Got it." He held out his hand.

Rolling her eyes, she walked past him and proceeded out of the door first. Hold his hand? Yeah, right.

A low chuckle drifted behind her. He could laugh all he wanted. She wasn't a public display kind of person. Plus, he was nothing to her. Just a guy. A guy she was helping out for the night. Nothing more would occur between them.

Elliot was in the living room when she walked back out. The concern still lingered in his eyes.

"I'll be ho—" She stopped herself before she said the word home. This wasn't her home. It never would be. "I'll be back later. I'm helping him with decorating or something."

A smile graced Elliot's face. "Have fun." His eyes grazed to Bentley, who stood behind her. "Take care of her, Bentley. Be careful. It's starting to snow a little harder."

"You got it, Chief. She'll be safe with me."

But would she? She could already feel the wall slipping a little as a warm hand touched the center of her back to urge her forward. Shaking off his hand, she erected the wall back in place and grabbed her coat from the closet. Maybe she'd keep her coat on the entire night if he insisted on touching her.

Better yet. No touching at all. She'd make that perfectly clear once they were alone in his truck. No need for Elliot to hear any of the sharp words that she was about to lay into him.

Bentley had no idea who he was dealing with.

But he'd know soon enough.

THE DOOR opposite of him slammed hard as he clicked his softly. He got it. He understood. She was upset. At him? At the world? He had no clue, but he got it.

He had those moments in his life.

Once when his uncle died of colon cancer. It came out of nowhere, and within a year, he was gone. It tore the entire family to pieces, but he felt it the worst. His uncle had been his hero from day one, the moment he understood what a firefighter did. That's the main reason he chose the profession he did. Because of his uncle.

Or the time he thought he had a chance at going pro in football, but apparently the scouts never agreed. He never got that recognition he wanted as he did in high school, loved by everyone. After his uncle passed, football didn't matter, anyway.

He could never forget how it felt trying to console his best friend, Aiden, losing the love of his life in a car accident. The pain and anguish every time he attempted to help his friend in his time of need and not being able to do a damn thing was almost too much to bear. Then to find out there was nothing he could've done. His friend had secrets no one knew about. Most people still didn't, except for him and a few select people.

So, yeah, he understood anger. He simply didn't know how to get past that with her, and he wanted to so badly. He wanted to wrap her in his arms and soothe the pain and anger away. In any way possible. If holding her all night would do the trick, then that's what he'd do. If only. He knew taking away pain wasn't that easy.

Glancing at her out of the corner of his eye as he started his truck, he didn't think she'd be receptive to that kind of gesture on his part, anyway.

"So—"

"Start keeping your hands to yourself, Romeo."

Bentley cocked a brow as he backed out of the driveway. He honestly had no clue what to say.

"Even if you're hanging a string of lights and I have to help and my hand accidentally brushes yours?" He grinned as he shifted into drive without looking at her. And he was oh so tempted to take a peek to see the irritated expression she probably wore.

"I don't like being touched. Keep your hands to yourself. Don't make me repeat myself."

Connecting eyes with her, just for a moment, he didn't miss the way her eyes glittered with desire. Did she mean what she said?

He wasn't the kind of man who didn't listen. If a woman didn't appreciate something, he wouldn't aggravate her.

That didn't mean he wouldn't tempt her to the ends of the Earth.

"You got it, my lady." He made sure to emphasize the words *my lady* as debonair as he could.

On cue, she scoffed under her breath. A chuckle escaped before he could stop himself. Boy, he loved to pester her a little too much.

He swung by the drive-thru at the best burger joint in town, and couldn't hold back a smile as she inhaled her hamburger. Apparently, she hadn't lied when she said she was hungry. Maybe that's all her attitude was about. Maybe he was overthinking things when it came to her.

They made it to the hotel with no more words spoken between them. Although it was lightly snowing out, it wasn't impeding the roads or visibility—yet.

They gathered in the ballroom and listened to Donna talk about how she wanted everything situated. Like last year, it took her a long time to explain everything. The entire time he couldn't stop glancing at Emma out of the corner of his eye. Each time he looked, he caught her looking back. It turned into him grinning like the Cheshire Cat and her cocking a brow with a severe frown.

He swore he saw a hint of desire mingled in with her irritation.

Or maybe it was wishful thinking on his part.

As soon as Donna told everyone to get to work, Emma walked away and started helping Gabby with hanging lights over the doorway to one entrance of the ballroom. Bentley figured she must've met her at some point because they started chatting as if they were old friends.

He decided to do what he did last year, arrange all the tables and chairs. Working with Gregory, they tackled the task easily. Then, with great reluctance, considering every time he tried to make eye contact with Emma and she refused to look his way, he let Marybeth finagle him into hanging lights with her on the opposite end of the ballroom.

"Who is she?"

Bentley didn't even bother to pretend ignorance. "A friend of Chief Duncan's. You don't even know her, Marybeth. Why the obvious dislike?"

She had the audacity to look shocked. "I never said I didn't like her. All I asked was who is she. You're so uptight, Bentley." Her expression softened as a hand landed on his shoulder. "I know it must be hard, but you're better off without Daphne."

Shrugging her hand off politely, he turned away from her fake sympathy she had plastered everywhere. The one thing he knew without a doubt was that Marybeth only cared about one thing—herself. He didn't believe for one second she felt any sort of sympathy for him.

Damn. He didn't realize he was so transparent with how much he coveted Daphne. And why? The more he thought about it, he couldn't figure out why he held her in such high regard. Yes, she was beautiful. Yes, she was kind, sweet, and thoughtful. Yes, he loved almost everything about her.

But...something was missing.

The challenge.

The kind of challenge Emma provided.

The more he compared the two, which he knew wasn't right, he couldn't help but like how much Emma challenged him on so many levels. She got his heart pumping, his nerves jangling, his stomach twisting with unease.

He didn't like those emotions, but he also couldn't help but feel addicted in a way. Like a sweet drug filling his body, refusing to give him peace until he had just a little more.

"Bentley...you know I mean that in a nice way."

"Yep." He was done with this conversation. Especially with Marybeth. He produced a grin he didn't want to and excused himself from her presence.

He almost felt bad walking away without finishing the string of lights they had been working on. His mind went into overdrive as he approached Emma. Enough keeping his distance. Enough letting her control the situation.

"Need help?"

She jerked at the sound of his voice, crouched near the bottom of the large Christmas tree that was centered in the middle of the room. Turning her head slightly, her hands still in position on the tree skirt she was obviously trying to arrange, she declined with a sharp shake of her head.

Refusing to be brushed off that easily, he crouched down next to her and grabbed a part of the tree skirt. His hand brushed hers, only a swift touch but enough that she flinched away.

"You didn't understand no?"

"I thought you were shaking your hair out of your face. You have a small strand in your eye." He couldn't resist. His hand reached up and brushed the strand of hair out of her eye and behind her ear.

A slight shiver coated her body at his soft touch. The desire he always swore he saw flared like a firework shooting into the sky. Then dimmed as if it never existed as she slapped his hand that still hung in the air near her ear.

"I said no touching."

He leaned closer and watched as her eyes dilated with pleasure. "My apologies, my lady."

Rolling her eyes, she shoved him playfully, knocking him off balance. He started to chuckle when he saw the small smile grace her face.

"You can go away now. I'm done arranging the tree skirt."

"What's next? I saw some mistletoes and wreathes in the box on the table. Do you want to help me hang those?" Heart pounding like a jackhammer going crazy, he waited impatiently for the only answer he would accept. Yes.

She looked away. "This is a gorgeous tree all decorated in white ornaments and lights. A beautiful white Christmas." Her voice trailed off as if she were reminiscing some memory she didn't want to share. Then she pointed between the branches hanging low to the floor. "Why is there a weird looking frog hiding right now?"

Bentley followed her finger and smiled wide. "I can't believe you found it. I have never found that thing in my life, and I've tried. Donna always hides that ornament in the tree, and during the party tomorrow, the first person to find it wins a fifty dollar gift card." He grinned crookedly. "Do you want to come to the party with me tomorrow? You could win the gift card."

Her head swiveled in his direction. "Well, that'd be like cheating. I know where it is."

"So, that was a...yes."

"That was a hard no." She laughed, a little too heartily in his opinion, stood up, and walked away.

His eyes landed on the frog hiding on a branch hidden quite well. He figured Emma would've never found it if she hadn't been crouched so low to the floor messing with the tree skirt. It was a small green frog, almost the same green as the tree branches, wearing a bright red Santa hat. Donna always hid it well. Even though the hat was bright red, people had to search hard to find it.

He found himself standing up and following her like a lost little puppy, or like an invisible string was attached between them and she kept reeling him in. She didn't like him. He got that impression loud and clear.

But part of her wanted to like him. He sensed it.

Or maybe he was a glutton for punishment.

Stopping next to the table where the boxes of mistletoes and wreathes sat, he couldn't hide his grin. She rolled her eyes as she grabbed the box and shoved it lightly into his stomach. "Lead the way." Her expression turned stern. "And. Keep. Your. Hands. To. Yourself."

His answer was a grin. A mischievous grin that he knew she saw right through.

6

Her hands curled around the warm mug a little tighter as she took a sip of the strong brew of coffee. Avoiding a conversation this morning obviously wasn't going to happen as Elliot took a seat next to her on the couch.

A cartoon droned on the television, although Laura had stepped out of the room to grab a bowl of cereal. They were officially alone. He had free rein to interrogate her about last night.

Not that she had anything to report. Bentley, besides the few times he touched the small of her back or their hands connected while attempting to hang some sort of decoration, was a gentleman. They even managed to laugh a few times, as if they were old friends or something.

She hated it.

She hated every time they shared a look and a tiny spark of desire zapped her in the heart. Feeling any emotion, especially the kind that would allow someone into her heart, was unacceptable. She couldn't handle the pain when they left. And they always left.

Like Elliot. He left.

"Did you have fun last night?"

Finally, he decided to speak. Just like she assumed, he wanted to talk about Bentley. Well, tough. She didn't.

Shrugging, she took a sip of coffee to avoid saying anything overly rude. Because only harsh, spiteful words wanted to unleash.

Elliot obviously got the message she didn't want to talk about it because he sighed heavily, but said nothing else on the matter.

"I went through those boxes you gave me from your father. None of that was my stuff. Did—"

"He wanted you to have that stuff." A small white lie wouldn't hurt anything. Her father never said specifically to give Elliot anything, but she knew he'd appreciate her father's baseball collection. It was either that or give it to the donation center. Or worse, throw it all away.

"Thank you for bringing it. I was always a little envious of his collection." Another soft sigh filtered out. "I'm worried about—"

"I should go." She abruptly stood up from the couch, almost sloshing coffee over the rim of her mug.

The surprised expression on Elliot's face made her heart ache. Ignoring the melancholy feeling, she attempted a smile. She knew it was fake. In all likelihood, Elliot knew it, too.

"Laura said Lynn's already at the bakery. She could use my help."

Elliot's features softened. The surprise and shock melted away. "We both appreciate all your help." He stood up slowly. "You can talk to me about anything. Remember that."

After a tight nod that she understood, she walked out of

the living room and to her room to get ready. Ten minutes later, her hands almost frozen the second she stepped outside into the blistering cold, she attempted to start her car.

Each time she tried to crank the engine, her hands got colder and colder. Her thin gloves did nothing to block out the cold. Thankfully, not much snow accumulated last night, but there was more snow in the forecast today. It hadn't started snowing yet.

"Come on, baby. Start for me."

The last thing she needed was Elliot stepping outside to see she was having car issues. He already worried too much about her. She didn't want that. She only wanted to enjoy her time here, then leave.

Maybe she should leave right now. Get the car started and keep driving right out of town.

After the third attempt, her beautiful car purred like a newborn kitten. Well, maybe like the runt of the litter, but still a beautiful sound, nonetheless.

She made her way to the bakery in short time and said a little prayer to her car before shutting it off that it better start for her when she finished at the bakery.

After a few short words with Lynn, she donned on an apron and shooed Lynn to the back of the bakery for her to finish creating her delicious treats she could bake with ease. She shuffled from counter to counter, filling orders, helping customers, wrapping treats, and worked her butt off until her legs wanted to cave in.

This business was no joke.

Two hours later, the door swung open, bringing in cold air and the last person she wanted to see.

Except, when a silky, sweet grin punctured his handsome face, she knew she was lying to herself. A little white lie. Boy, those lies could do more damage than she realized.

"How's my favorite lady that loves to glare at me?"

A chuckle escaped before she could stop herself. The things he said shouldn't make her laugh. Shouldn't make her heart soar, her hands shake, her mind think maybe she could be happy for once.

"What do you want, Bentley? A box of cookies? A cake? Some doughnuts?"

"Your company would be nice. Can I get that wrapped with one of those fancy red ribbons?"

Her eyes followed his gaze to the ribbon sitting on the counter behind her. Delicious, naughty scenarios pelted her mind as she stared at the bright, vibrant ribbon. He wanted to wrap her up? Yes, please.

No! What was she thinking?

Swiveling her gaze back to his, she intensified her glare. The irritating man grinned wider. "Go away. I had enough of you last night."

"So, does that mean you're not coming to the Christmas party with me tonight?" The puppy dog expression on his face almost made her want to cave. Almost.

But she wasn't going regardless. Elliot even invited her. She declined politely, because going to the party would bring lots of curiosity and questions she didn't want to answer.

Who was she? How did she know Elliot? Why was she here? How long was she staying?

It was nobodies damn business. Not even Bentley's.

"I'm not into Christmas parties. Sorry."

He clapped his hands and rubbed them together excitedly. "That's great news. Excellent."

Frowning, she couldn't figure out why he sounded so

excited by her answer. She expected him to be upset and fight her every step of the way.

Her eyes narrowed. The mischievous glint in his eyes didn't bode well for her. "What? Quit staring at me like that."

He leaned forward. "Like what? Like you look beautiful? Like I want to lick off the dusting of powdered sugar that's on your cheek?" He leaned even closer, his eyes lowering to her mouth. "That you've been on my mind all night and morning?"

The beating of her heart, that started rapidly beating the moment he called her beautiful, started to hammer like crazy when his eyes shifted back to her. The amount of passion gazing at her almost made her knees buckle. No man had ever looked at her with such intensity.

"I'm hanging out with my friends, Aiden and Theresa, tonight. Join me?"

By the heat in his eyes, the passion, she found herself saying the only thing she could think of. "Okay."

She regretted it the moment she said it.

A devilish smile that should've scared her, but didn't, warped his face. Without missing a beat, a warm hand wrapped around her neck and pulled her closer. Soft lips connected with hers.

The kiss was short and brief, but oh so sweet. A low, disappointing moan left her mouth as he pulled away, his hand still pressed to her neck, his fingers softly rubbing.

"I'll pick you up around eight."

With his warm hand on her body, she couldn't find the words to argue. Then his lips were touching hers once again. This time a little more insistent, a little rougher, as if he knew she wanted to resist him every step of the way.

Letting her go slowly, the fierce passion still in his eyes, he smiled and started for the door.

"No more kissing, Bentley."

He stopped at the door and turned toward her. "Sound like you mean it and I just might." He winked and walked out.

Oh, boy.

The most annoying man was making it so easy to fall for him.

Damn him, and damn her emotions.

She'd need to fortify her defenses before tonight if she wanted to survive.

"LEAVING SO SOON?"

Bentley stopped in his tracks and debated whether he should keep walking away without turning around. Swiveling slowly, he produced a grin for Chief Duncan. "I promised Aiden and Theresa I'd come over tonight."

Chief Duncan took a sip of his champagne as he stepped closer. Close enough where no one else would hear their conversation. Bentley had a strong feeling he needed that at the moment. Because Chief Duncan's smile slowly died. He knew right away what Chief Duncan wanted to say.

He was going to warn him off Emma.

Beautiful, aggravating, sometimes sweet, Emma.

The Christmas music lightly playing in the background dimmed to a low hum as Bentley prepared for the brutal blow of being told to back off.

Not good enough once again. The story of his life, apparently.

"What's going on?"

Bentley cocked a brow as if confused. "I'm making an appearance like Chief Downing asked me to. Honestly, I'd rather be at Aiden and Theresa's already."

"It's a great party. You did a good job decorating." Elliot's eyes turned suspicious. "But you know I wasn't talking about the party."

He sighed, rubbing a hand over his face as his eyes fell to the floor.

"I'm not dumb, Bentley. It might have been fifteen years since I've seen Emma, but she's like a niece to me. I was close to her father. Since he's not here to protect her, I will."

His eyes shot up. "Protect her? From me? I didn't realize I was such a bad guy. I guess running into a burning building makes me a danger."

Maybe that was uncalled for, but since that fire a few nights ago, he felt like everyone thought he did something wrong. Oh, they saw him as a hero, but an idiotic one. Unofficially suspended. Odd looks from some of the townsfolk. Now this.

"I wasn't talking about the fire. I'm talking about your feelings for Daphne. It's no secret. I find it somewhat suspicious you're suddenly showering Emma with all this attention." Chief Duncan leaned closer. "Maybe I'm overstepping my boundaries, but I don't care. I won't let anyone hurt her, especially when I think something is bothering her."

Bentley's anger depleted slightly. He couldn't fault the chief for drawing conclusions that Emma was a distraction since Daphne was soon to be married. Honestly, since he met Emma, Daphne barely filtered through his mind. So strange, yet refreshing. The anticipation, the new desire, the giddy feeling of meeting someone new was so invigorating.

"There's something about her, Chief..." He almost avoided looking him in the eye. "But my intentions are good.

This has nothing to do with Daphne. She's the first woman in a long time that actually...gets me excited. I look forward to our...conversations." That word was better than battles. Because, boy, they could go back and forth with ease. He wouldn't necessarily call them tame conversations.

Chief Duncan laid a tender hand on his shoulder. "She's had it rough. She lost her mother at a young age. Now her father passed away recently. As far as I know, she has no other family in her life. She might act tough, but she's vulnerable right now. She's more sensitive than she portrays. I made the mistake of leaving and not keeping in touch, but life got in the way." He sighed. "She doesn't live here, Bentley. I have no idea how long she plans to stay. Actually, I don't know her plans for anything. She doesn't like to talk about it."

"I won't hurt her, Chief. This isn't a game to me. I like her."

The chief squeezed his shoulder. "Then you have my blessing."

Bentley smiled. "I appreciate it."

He said goodbye to the chief and a few other people on his way out of the ballroom and headed quickly for his truck. The sooner he picked up Emma, the better he'd feel. The chief didn't realize it, but he revealed some things about Emma that he wasn't aware of. Despite knowing a bit of her background, he wouldn't be bringing it up. He wanted to hear everything from her lips, if she was willing to share. He didn't have seriously high hopes she would.

Breaking her defenses was proving harder than he imagined, but he wasn't prepared to give up yet.

As he knocked on Chief Duncan's door, waiting somewhat impatiently for Emma, he knew it might take longer than the holidays to penetrate through her defenses.

Not good news.

Especially if she planned to leave as soon as Christmas ended.

His full on Bentley charm wasn't working. Maybe he'd ask Aiden for some tips.

The door swung open.

Emma had on an old ratty T-shirt and a pair of sweats. Her hair was in its usual ponytail and she wore no makeup.

Beautiful.

Every inch of her.

"Oh, you were serious earlier?"

He grinned to hide the disappointment in her words. Maybe he was wasting his time. Would he ever be able to get past her defenses?

Did that kiss mean nothing to her?

Because he'd never felt so alive kissing a woman before.

In fact, he wanted to kiss her breathless again. Right now.

Except the glower on her face didn't look promising.

"You look beautiful."

She snorted.

"I'm not in the habit of lying." His grin widened. He wouldn't be shut out by this woman. "Grab your jacket."

Her eyes bulged as she waved a hand up and down. "You want me to go dressed like this?"

"I want you to come with me and have some fun tonight. I already said you look beautiful. It's your choice if you want to change."

He meant every word. She was beautiful no matter what she wore. Makeup, no makeup. Nothing could sway her beauty.

Her frown started to disappear as a new light entered

her eyes. Perhaps he was making a bit more headway than he realized.

A shiver coated her body. Whether from the cold seeping in from outside or from the sudden bliss he spotted in her eyes, he didn't know. But he stepped closer, wrapped a hand around her neck like he did earlier in the bakery, and rested his forehead against hers.

"I don't know what's happening here between us, but I'd like to find out. What about you? Are you up for the challenge?"

She stiffened. He knew right away she wouldn't be able to resist him. To resist any kind of challenge.

"I want to change."

Bentley figured she meant her clothes, but part of him thought maybe she meant a part of herself. If he had his way, he wouldn't change a single part of her.

Pressing his lips lightly to hers, he lingered for a moment, savoring the softness of her lips, the sweetness of her taste. He wanted to forget about leaving and take the pleasure developing between them to a higher level. Knowing that wasn't possible, he intensified the kiss briefly, then let go of her.

"You won't regret anything."

Her eyes twinkled with delight. "I have a feeling I already do."

7

Her eyes widened in surprise as Bentley pulled into a long driveway and the house came into view. Decorated with bright white lights and Santa pulling a sleigh on the roof, the house looked positively magical. She wasn't a person who found things *magical*.

Her dad used to love to decorate the house for Christmas. He went all out with beautiful, colorful Christmas trees that twinkled all night to gaudy, outrageous blow-up decorations like huge snow globes and different scenes from the North Pole.

Tears almost threatened to flow as memory after memory assaulted her.

A soft voice whispered next to her, which broke up the attack and reined in her emotions. "It looks awesome, but it was a bitch to set up."

Bentley's sweet, low laughter sent her heart into a tiny pitter-pattering frenzy. The kind of frenzy she had been experiencing too much since meeting him. But his voice did the trick. It stopped the wayward memories from ruining the night.

She turned to him and smiled. “You did a great job. Did you also decorate your house?”

A strange twinkle entered his eyes. “I’d be more than happy to show you later.”

“That wasn’t quite a yes or a no.”

He shrugged in a boyish, yet smooth manner. The man was trying to entice her. To get her alone. To ravish her, maybe?

After the few kisses they shared, she was more than ready to be ravished. She didn’t want to like this guy, but the more time she spent with him, the easier and easier it was getting to let down her shield and let him in.

Of course, disaster sat on the horizon if she truly let him in. But letting him graze the surface wouldn’t do any harm.

She’d have fun these next two weeks and then she’d leave.

No harm having a little fun.

A wicked grin emerged.

“Should I be nervous? That look has me slightly nervous.”

She chuckled. “You should be nervous.”

Then she exited the vehicle before he could respond. Another laugh escaped when she couldn’t get his shocked expression out of her mind.

Oh, man, she had so much fun messing with him. He wasn’t like other men that couldn’t take a little teasing.

Pussies. Every single man that ever chided her for being a little too bold, a little too rash.

Bentley, so far, had handled everything she threw at him. It was refreshing to spar with a guy and know he wouldn’t have his feelings hurt like a little pansy.

A squeal rented the air as a strong pair of hands wrapped around her waist and lifted her in a circle. Bentley twirled her a few times, then set her down and twisted her in his arms until she was facing him. His hazel eyes glowed a brilliant color as desire sparkled like the star on top of a Christmas tree.

"What was that for?"

"Maybe I want you a little nervous, too. I might pick you up at random times and twirl you..." His eyes lowered to her lips. "Or kiss you. I can't decide how I want to torture you yet."

"Yeah, those kisses were torturous. I almost—"

Her words were cut off as his lips claimed hers. Not like those other kisses that she thought had been passionate. No. *This* kiss was passionate. Wild and fierce. She couldn't contain the moan that slipped from her lips as his arms tightened around her.

His tongue swept in and tussled with hers, as they enjoyed doing with words. They sparred back and forth like two warriors dueling to the death. The intense kiss awakened so many emotions she worked so hard at suppressing. They broke free like a bundle of balloons floating separately into the sky.

Unlike how it started, deep and powerful, it ended slow and sensually. Just like she wanted to cry in the truck, another tear almost appeared when his lips drifted away.

"I can't seem to stop kissing you. It's kind of fun."

She slapped his shoulder playfully. "Only kind of?"

"Well, it ranks up there with watching a football game with my friends. That's kind of fun. But it's more exciting to actually go to the game."

"Did you just use a euphemism with sex and football? Like sex would be more exciting than a simple kiss?"

"That sounds idiotic and I'd never do something so idiotic." He cocked a brow as if waiting for her to challenge that statement. Because he knew he was wrong. Laughter filled the cold night air. "Okay. That was stupid. You can call me an idiot."

"Well, you are, but you're a cute idiot." She patted his shoulder, then slipped out of his arms and headed for the door.

Not only was she starting to freeze from the temperature outside, but she could only handle so many emotions hitting her at once. While she couldn't quite determine what that conversation they had was about, she knew it scared her.

That was the problem with Bentley. He scared her. He scared her so much she wasn't sure how she would survive when she eventually left. He pulled the emotions out of her so easily. She couldn't keep letting him do that.

Blowing out a breath, she tried to wash those feelings away, determined to have fun. She would have fun these next two weeks. She would not allow her fear to hold her back.

Unexpectedly, an arm slid around her waist as she stopped in front of the door. The simple gesture had her heart beating like mad. She shouldn't secretly love how his touch made her crave more, but she did.

"So you think I'm cute, huh?" he asked with a chuckle as he pressed the doorbell with his free hand. His other hand was securely wrapped around her waist. She wouldn't wish it away for the world.

"Kind of."

Deep, masculine laughter filled her soul as Bentley reacted to her comeback.

The door swung open. Even though she didn't know the

man standing before her, she couldn't remove the silly grin on her face.

She felt so alive. She hadn't felt like this in a long time.

All because of one man.

Bentley.

"What's so funny? Don't leave me hanging," the somewhat cute guy said. He looked handsome in a sweet, adorable way. As she assessed him from head to toe, dressed in jeans and a shirt with bare feet, she decided he was good-looking.

But he didn't hold a candle to Bentley.

"Dude, it was one of those things where you had to be there. Sorry." Bentley's hand tightened on her waist. She found the gesture a little too endearing to her battered heart. "This is Emma." His mouth lowered closer to her ear. "Emma, this is my best friend Aiden."

Shivering from the warmth of his breath, she tried to keep a smile on her face when she really wanted to close her eyes and savor how her name left his mouth so erotically.

"It's nice to meet you, Emma. Come on in. Theresa made some hot chocolate martinis." Aiden closed the door and gestured for them to lead the way. "My wife sucks at making coffee, so beware, Emma, but she makes a mean martini."

Emma glanced behind her shoulder as her brow rose. "Does your wife know you say such things?" Because she would not appreciate her husband saying something like that about her behind her back.

She didn't like anyone saying things behind her back. She learned the hard way what kind of friends she had. Like Ashley, who was never truly her best friend.

"What things?"

Emma turned toward the soft voice. A beautiful woman

with the brightest green eyes she had ever seen looked at her confused, yet not concerned.

Aiden walked around them, wrapped an arm around his wife, and grinned. “I was telling Emma to be careful if you make the coffee.” He kissed her gently. “But you know I’ll drink anything you make, terrible or not.”

Theresa lightly laughed. “Yesterday’s batch wasn’t that bad.”

“This is true. I enjoyed it,” Bentley replied.

Emma twisted her head, the shock still registering. Bentley saw her obvious confusion and stepped closer, wrapping an arm around her waist as Aiden had done with Theresa. She wanted to feel embarrassed by his clear show of possession, but her giddy heart only soared higher into a happiness she hadn’t felt in forever.

“We’re not being mean when we say she makes terrible coffee. We love Theresa no matter what, and we’ll drink even the strongest sludge she makes.” Bentley’s soft tone slid down her spine in delicious tingles. She shouldn’t be feeling this way, but when he held her so close, speaking so tenderly, she couldn’t help but shiver with delight.

“Hey, these jokers don’t even know if I make it on purpose sometimes,” Theresa said with a laugh.

“It doesn’t matter. I’ll still drink it.” Aiden kissed her again.

Emma relaxed, the tension slowly releasing, as she understood Theresa didn’t find any offense by the things they were saying. Bentley must’ve felt the change because his hand lightly squeezed her waist in response. He didn’t kiss her like she suddenly wished for him to do, but that simple gesture helped the rest of her tension dissipate.

“Let’s grab those martinis and then get this party started. Can you play cards, Emma?” Aiden asked.

"A bit."

She wasn't about to confess she knew how to play well. Her dad taught her everything he thought she should know. Cards had been on the top of the list.

"Oh, boy," Bentley muttered.

"What?" Aiden asked as his brows dropped into a frown.

"I think we're about to have our asses handed to us." He tilted his head toward her as his signature silky grin touched his lips. "Aren't we?"

She shrugged. "Are you?"

"Let the games begin, sweetheart."

The tender way Bentley said sweetheart was enough to melt her frozen heart into a big puddle of water.

Oh, yeah. The games were about to begin.

If she wasn't careful, she'd lose her heart and all.

"OKAY. HOW DID YOU KNOW?"

Bentley jumped, embarrassed he let Aiden make him flinch. The fridge door closed behind him as he twisted the cap off the beer bottle. "Know what? I have no idea what you're talking about."

Aiden grinned as he leaned against the counter. "That Emma would know how to play cards so well. If we were playing with real money, we'd all be in the hole pretty badly. She's a card shark."

Laughter filled the kitchen as they both couldn't hold it in.

"It's the way she said it."

The grin didn't leave Aiden's face, but the concern deepened in his eyes. "What's going on here, Bentley? I like her. I really do. But just a few days ago, you were pining over Daphne, and now you're latching onto Emma pretty hard."

Wow. For the second time tonight, someone wanted to question him about his feelings and actions toward Emma. Like he was some sort of bad guy out to do her harm. And from his best friend. That hurt. That hurt way more than Chief Duncan calling him out.

"Do you have a point?" He didn't bother to hide his irritation as his brows glowered and the words came out harsh.

Aiden's smile vanished, but the concern was still prominent. "I'm not saying you're out to hurt her or anything. I'm worried about you. I know Daphne—"

"Enough about Daphne." He barely controlled the urge to shout. The last thing he needed was the ladies rushing to the kitchen to find out why they were arguing.

Did he have a massive crush on Daphne? Yep. He wouldn't deny it.

Was he over it? Surprisingly, yes. Because every time his mind conjured an image of a woman, it was Emma's beautiful face, not Daphne's.

Why? He couldn't explain it, not even to himself.

But he knew Emma was special, and he wanted to find out how much. He wanted to see if they were compatible. He wanted to see if they could make whatever was brewing between them into a relationship.

So yeah, if he suddenly wanted to let his crush for Daphne disappear, that was his business.

"Emma is..." Bentley shrugged, unsure of how to explain properly. "She's special. And if you can't see that, that's not my problem." He stepped closer, lowering his voice. "Don't you dare make her feel like she's not good enough."

Aiden's hands shot up in an innocent gesture, as if

surrendering. “Whoa. I never said she wasn’t good enough. I like her. She’s great. I want to see you move on. It’s just...it came out of nowhere.”

“Yeah, and you proposed to Theresa within two weeks of dating. Talk about coming out of nowhere. Sometimes shit happens and you go with the flow. What’s so wrong with that?”

A slow grin appeared. “Absolutely nothing. If you’re happy, I’m happy.”

Bentley matched Aiden’s silly grin. “Well, okay, then.”

“Fine.”

“Good.”

Aiden chuckled. “Perhaps we should join the ladies now.”

Bentley took another sip of beer as he followed Aiden out of the kitchen. He had one martini and now this beer. He’d stop after this one, especially since he was driving. Emma still had her martini in front of her, slowly sipping. He didn’t mind if she let go and had a few more. As long as she was having a good time, he was okay with anything.

When he took his seat and connected eyes with her, he couldn’t stop the goofy grin that touched his lips. A sweet smile punctured her beautiful face as her eyes twinkled with mischief.

Oh, she was definitely having fun.

Although he was getting his ass handed to him at cards, he didn’t care. She could school him any day in cards, as long as that gorgeous smile stayed on her face.

He suddenly wanted to leave. He wanted to get her alone and show her how much he loved that smile of hers.

“We should make this next game interesting,” Emma said as she stared naughtily at him.

For a brief moment, he thought she wanted to turn this game extremely interesting. A kind of interesting where some people might lose articles of clothing. He was all for her losing every single thing she was wearing, just not with other people in the room.

"How so?" Theresa asked with an excited tone.

"Well…" Emma didn't tear her eyes away from his, even though she was answering Theresa's question. "Loser has to grant the winner a wish." She turned to Theresa. "Like a Christmas wish or something. We each deal a hand and play one-on-one with one person. We can all do one round." She shrugged as she lowered her eyes to the table. "It sounds silly now that I say it."

"I like it," Aiden said. "I'll even say you can be the only dealer, Emma, even though I have a feeling you'll win each hand."

Emma's eyes lifted as she chuckled. "I didn't win them all."

"Close enough," Aiden replied with a low chuckle.

"Let's do it." Bentley rubbed his hands together.

After that, it was settled. Emma started with Aiden, dealing out five cards to both of them, winning quite easily. Theresa went next, and also lost fairly quickly.

When Emma started to deal the cards, her eyes never left his as each card hit the table.

"Ready to lose?"

He wanted to box up that sweet, sensual smile in her eyes to take out later and savor it. Playing this Christmas wish game was worth it simply to see that smile. "Sweetheart, there's only going to be one loser here, and it won't be me."

He would win this hand. He hadn't won a single hand

tonight. Talk about being a loser. He wouldn't say he was terrible at cards, but when faced against Emma, he had lost every single time. Her eyes said he'd be losing again.

Game on, sweetheart.

When he won a Christmas wish, he'd make good use of it. Somehow. He just wasn't sure how yet.

Grabbing one card at a time, he tried to keep his expression neutral as four diamonds appeared before him. Two high cards with two low cards, but diamonds. He needed one more for a flush.

This was his first decent hand of the night.

"How many would you like?"

Laying one card face down, he couldn't help the silly grin that touched his lips. "One, please."

She chuckled as she tossed the card to the side and then dealt him one card. "You're a terrible card player. You obviously have a good hand." She lifted her eyes in a playful manner as she laughed. "Not as good as mine."

She tossed two cards out of her hand into the pile on the side and dealt herself two more cards.

"Well, let's see what you got."

Her eyes sparkled with victory. "You first."

"How about on the count of three, we lay them together?"

She nodded.

Aiden piped in. "I'll count."

They listened intently as Aiden counted down to one, never taking their eyes off each other. As soon as he finished, they turned over their hands, still maintaining eye contact.

"Well, shit."

Bentley jerked his gaze from Emma to Aiden. "What?"

"You won your first hand of the night, buddy."

His eyes flew to the table where his beautiful flush, since he managed to get that last diamond, beat her three of a kind.

Hot damn.

He did win.

"A Christmas wish just for me." He rubbed his hands gleefully.

Instead of seeing disappointment, Emma's eyes sparkled with delight. "And what is your wish?"

"When I know, you'll know."

He couldn't wish for something simple. It had to be the best wish he could think of. A unique wish. Something that would surprise and shock her, yet make that beautiful smile of hers appear.

Her cheeks flushed a bright shade of red before she averted eye contact and looked at Aiden and Theresa, who sat close together. "Can I have my wish from you two already?"

"Of course," Theresa said as she glanced at him with a sly grin. He didn't even want to interpret why she looked at him like that.

Obviously, Aiden and Theresa were having too much fun at his expense. Probably because he rarely dated, and now he was suddenly showing a strong interest in a woman.

"I would love if you could help me find a great gift for Elliot and Lynn. Laura, too. I'm staying until Christmas and I want to get all of them a present, but I'm so clueless."

Theresa smiled gently. "That doesn't have to be your Christmas wish. I would've helped you do that no matter what."

"Thank you. I want to get them a great present since they've been so nice letting me stick around for a while."

From there, Theresa and Emma launched into a conversation about the perfect gifts. Aiden offered his opinion at times.

Bentley sat there listening and watching. And thinking.

His Christmas wish had to be perfect.

8

Emma rotated her shoulders for a few seconds before grabbing another plastic container and then counted out ten cookies. Not plain old boring cookies, but Christmas cookies: Santas, reindeers, snowmen, Christmas trees. They were decorated with the most delicious icing she had ever tasted.

Lynn had talent. There was no doubt about it. Hell, she was such an excellent baker, Emma would pay good money to have her goodies shipped to her.

When she left.

The thought of leaving hurt more than she cared to admit.

But she couldn't stay here.

Could she?

While last night had been fun, it wasn't a night that would forever change her life. Just because Bentley was attentive and sweet and made her laugh every other minute didn't mean he wanted her for the long haul.

There was no future for them.

There was no future for her with anyone.

But it didn't mean she couldn't have fun. Which was what she told herself when she agreed to hang out with him again...tonight.

A slow smile graced her face. No matter how hard she tried, she couldn't erase the goofy grin. Crazy how the simple thought of seeing him put her in a giddy mood.

She missed the annoying man. Oh, boy, could he be so annoying.

A little laugh escaped.

Like how he couldn't stop rubbing it in he won one game. One.

But out of every game they played, he won the most important one.

A Christmas wish.

The way he looked at her, she swore he was going to ask for it last night before he dropped her off. But nothing. He didn't ask her to his house. He didn't ask for a wish. He simply walked her to the door, kissed her sweetly, and waited on the porch until she walked inside and closed the door.

A pure gentleman.

She wasn't used to those kinds of men. Most of the time, she hooked up with losers going nowhere in life, or men looking for a fun time between the sheets. She dated one sweet guy in high school, but it had been a silly high school romance. It never went very far.

"What's with the smile?"

Jerking her attention from the cookies laid out on the table to Lynn standing on the other side of the table, her smile slowly died.

"What smile?"

The way Lynn pursed her lips playfully said she wasn't

fooled. "So I didn't have a chance to ask you this morning how last night went. Did you have fun?"

Her eyes fell to the cookies as she shrugged. "Yeah, it wasn't bad."

"Good. I'm glad."

She lifted her gaze once again, curious why Lynn didn't probe more. People always loved to get in her business, nagging, asking questions until she finally lost her patience and said things she meant but shouldn't have said.

Her father always said she had her mother's temper. She took that as a compliment.

"Do you want to pick out the movie tonight?"

She knew Lynn was trying to be nice, but now she had to answer the question and divulge her plans for the night. Which she knew she would've had to eventually, but she had hoped to spring it on them a few minutes before Bentley arrived so she didn't have to answer any questions.

Or maybe she should cancel on him and say she'd love to pick out the movie tonight.

Decisions. Decisions.

Have fun for the short time she's here with a sexy, handsome, aggravating man? Or enjoy her time with Elliot and his family and protect her heart from all things enticing?

"I...uh..." She took a deep breath. "I have plans tonight."

That knowing smile touched Lynn's features once again. "He's a good guy. I hope you have fun."

She shrugged as she lowered her gaze back to the cookies, yet didn't grab any to continue packing them.

"Change isn't easy. Elliot tells me you were close with your dad. I'm so blessed to have met Elliot and Gregory, and Elliot has been the best father figure to Laura. My parents disowned me when I got pregnant with Laura. That was the hardest thing I ever went through...and losing Laura's father..." A heavy sigh released. "But you can get through it. We're here for you. I think you know that, otherwise, why did you come?"

Her head popped up. "I came to drop off those boxes to Elliot."

"Is that the only reason? I get it, Emma. You're scared. You're unsure. I went through all of these emotions when I moved away from my parents and built a new life. It's possible to move on and be happy. Even before I met Elliot, I was happy. Because I kept pushing on."

Her brows puckered. "Are you saying I'm not?"

Lynn jerked back by her sudden harsh tone. "That's not what I said. I apologize if I overstepped my boundaries. I want you to know I'm here for you. We all are. This town bands together when someone is in need. Remember that."

"I'm not a part of this town."

Lynn shrugged nonchalantly, even though her eyes held an enormous amount of concern. "But you could be. Ultimately, it's your choice."

With those parting words, Lynn walked through the double swinging doors, leaving Emma to her own turbulent thoughts.

Could she stay and be a part of this town?

Did she even want to?

Bentley's charming face punctured her thoughts.

She might be unsure of the direction she should take, but he made her decision sway a little toward what the obvious answer should be.

Staying.

The rest of the day progressed with no other awkward conversations or outbursts by her. With time to herself to think over everything said, she realized she snapped a little too harshly at Lynn, whom she knew was only trying to help.

Apologizing wasn't a strong suit of hers. Never had been.

While getting ready for Bentley to pick her up, she debated, even practiced different ways in the mirror how to say sorry. It all sounded dumb and insincere.

She was sorry. To an extent. She appreciated the thought of Lynn attempting to help, but she didn't like people getting in her business. She never had. And that's exactly how she felt.

Instead of apologizing, she said a quick goodbye and waited for Bentley on the front porch. The cold seeped into her lonely bones, shivering from the brisk wind, wishing Bentley would hurry up. He was on time yesterday, so she didn't think she'd have to wait much longer.

Elliot had given her a strange look when she headed for the foyer, but thankfully, didn't stop her. He didn't ask questions. He didn't berate her for speaking to Lynn the way she had, assuming Lynn told him. He gave her the space she desperately needed.

Right on cue, Bentley's truck pulled into the driveway. She didn't wait for him to act like a gentleman and step out of the truck; she ran quickly to the passenger side and hopped in, almost before he could put it in park.

"Eager to see me? I like this."

A laugh escaped as she averted eye contact. She didn't want him to see how eager she actually was about seeing him. "Dream on, lover boy."

Bentley chuckled as he backed out of the driveway and headed down the block. Less than a minute later, he pulled into another driveway. The house was small, one story, with two large bushes in front with white twinkling lights brightening the entrance. A string of icicle lights hung from the gutters.

"Wow, boring. I expected more lights."

A deep, boisterous laugh echoed between them. "I love your honesty. It's so refreshing." He winked as her laughter joined his. "I barely had time to put this up. Come on. Let me show you the awesome tree inside."

She chuckled, then followed him to the doorstep, shivering once again from the brutal cold, and a little from the nerves that suddenly attacked her.

What was there to be nervous about? No big deal. She'd been to a guy's house before.

Bentley let her step through the door first after unlocking it, then closed and shut it. Lights were already ablaze as she shrugged out of her coat. He grabbed her coat and hung it up in the small closet near the door.

"You live really close to Elliot's. I totally could've walked here."

He hung his coat next to hers. "True, you could've. But what kind of gentleman would I be if I let you walk?"

And Bentley was a gentleman. She couldn't dispute that.

Right now, that's not what she wanted.

She wanted a bad boy.

She wanted to unleash her anger and anguish that had been filling her veins for the longest time.

She wanted Bentley to erase the pain for a few minutes.

Because no matter how many times she tried to make the pain disappear, it always reappeared within seconds.

Closing the closet door, he turned around. She didn't hesitate as she wrapped her arms around his neck and planted a quick kiss to his lips. The first kiss she ever initiated between them.

"Show me your bedroom."

❄

The kiss caught him off guard, but that didn't mean he let go of her. If anything, his hands tightened around her waist.

He didn't plan much for the evening other than tossing in a movie and munching on some snacks. His instincts had said he should take things slowly so he didn't frighten her away. And here she was throwing herself in his arms, demanding he move this show along.

Part of him didn't think this was the right plan. Even as he held her, he could see the pain in her eyes.

She was using him.

"Bentley..."

His name slid out of her mouth in an erotic whisper. Ignoring the sexual tension between them wouldn't be easy if he put a stop to it. He didn't want to.

But he also didn't want her to use him to block out whatever was bothering her.

The desire slowly started to disappear from her eyes when he didn't respond. He couldn't have that.

Emma was different. She didn't express her feelings in the same way others did. He knew there was a lingering pain hidden inside, but she wouldn't share until she was ready.

Wasn't his life a complete mess at the moment? Daphne getting married and everyone feeling sorry for him because they knew he pined over her for way too long. Getting reamed out by his boss for saving a puppy. Some of the townsfolk looking at him as if he was a loose cannon because he ran into a burning building after being told not to.

He needed to release some pain as well.

They could do it together. Screw the consequences. He had no doubt there would be plenty of consequences.

Before the want died in her eyes, he slid his hands to her ass and scooped her up. Her legs immediately went around his waist as a small delighted squeal left her mouth. He started to pepper tiny kisses to her neck as he made his way down the hallway to his bedroom.

"I hope you don't run into a wall."

"Are you saying I can't effectively kiss you and walk at the same time?" he asked as his tongue traced from her neck to her ear, slowly and deliciously. She tasted so damn sweet.

"Maybe."

She screamed playfully when he tossed her in the air. Her eyes widened with surprise and laughter filled the air as she landed on the soft king-size bed.

"That wasn't nice." Her eyes begged him to come closer.

"Teasing me has consequences. You have been warned."

Her finger traced her bottom lip, then slowly made a path down her chest and to the edge of her shirt. His body roared to life at the tantalizing show before him. The little minx was doing more than simple teasing. She was enticing to the point of madness.

"You don't scare me, Bentley."

He pounced quickly, jumping on the bed and hovering over her body before she could escape. Another enchanting laugh left her lips. If he could, he'd listen to her laugh all day, every day. She had the sweetest, most adorable laugh he had ever heard.

His finger trailed the same path she took, except when he got to the edge of her shirt, he pulled it up and over her head. A black lacy bra covered her ample breasts, her rosy nipples perky and waiting for him to devour. He didn't wait either, clamping his mouth over a taut nipple and sucking hard.

She arched into him at the touch, her hands grabbing him on the back, squeezing his shirt tightly.

He lightly bit her nipple before backing away, meeting her gaze. "I might not scare you, but I plan to keep you on your toes."

Her answer was to bite her lip as she yanked his shirt off. Then her hands started to trace his chest. Up, then down. Her hands circled low around the edge of his jeans. Teasing a little too much for his tastes. She was asking for trouble. Her eyes glittered with evil, delicious intent.

He might've had reservations out in the foyer, but none of those worries lingered now.

He wanted Emma.

He wanted her so badly.

His lips touched her neck, his tongue swirling, his teeth grazing, his body pressing into her as he started the delicious assault on her body. She had no choice but to move her hands from his chest and wrap them around him instead. Her fingers grazing his back drove the fire in him even higher.

He slowly made his way down, removing her bra with ease, then he took his time treasuring first one breast, then the other. Her movements, her low moans, all made his cock twitch with happy anticipation. He wanted her now.

But he continued his descent, unbuttoning the snap of her jeans, and removed them as quickly as possible. A black lacy thong was the only thing that stood between him and what he wanted.

A slow grin emerged as he pictured her dressing up before waiting for him outside, which he was curious why she had been waiting on the porch. He'd have to ask her about that later. He almost did in the truck, but knew it had been bad timing. Something was bothering her and he knew he wouldn't have gotten a decent answer out of her.

Did she wear this thong for him?

Because it was now his.

He grabbed the tiny straps of the thong on both sides as he looked into her gorgeous chocolate brown eyes. Her eyes widened in shock as he tore off the thong with one smooth move. He winked, then tossed it behind him.

Before she could slash him with her rough words, he bent down and claimed her. His tongue dove in the most sensitive part of her body, swirling, dancing, and devouring her until low, throaty moans started to fill the semi-dark room. Only a hint of light filtered in from the hallway. It was enough to see how her face lit up with pleasure as he took his time savoring every moment.

A hand grabbed his hair, pulling, rubbing, and demanding he continue until she was sated with bliss. Oh, he had no intention of stopping. She tasted so sweet and delicious, he wasn't sure he'd ever get enough of her. This one night would never be enough.

That thought sent a sharp, brutal pain to his heart, as a finger joined his tongue, increasing her pleasure so much her moans became a little louder.

He didn't want to lose her. He didn't want to say goodbye after the holidays ended.

But he had no idea how to keep her here. With him.

Finding the right spot, as her hands tightened in his hair, he suckled harder, another finger dipping inside and increasing its pace until she tightened all around him and let out a low murmured scream. Her body lightly shook as her orgasm took over.

When he drained every last ounce of bliss out of her, he

looked up with a sly grin as he slid back up her body and to her lips, planting a light kiss upon them. "That's what you get for teasing me."

A smile lit up her beautiful face. "Oh, yeah. I can't help myself. I'm a naughty girl."

He liked this naughty side of her. Honestly, he would do that again and again just because he enjoyed it.

Her hands slid down his back. "Why are you still half dressed?"

"A form of torture?" He cocked an eyebrow as she slapped his ass.

Chuckling, he quickly removed his pants and boxers, reaching over to his nightstand to grab a condom. His eyes met hers as he opened the package and slid on the condom. The desire shining within her beautiful depths before compared nothing to what he saw now. Pure, unabashed bliss.

Without saying a word, afraid he'd say the wrong thing, he slid into her with ease. They both sighed with contentment. Almost at the same time.

He found it reassuring, as if telling him she felt the same exact thing.

They were meant to be together.

The thought hit him square in the chest. Quick and forceful.

She was his.

She might not realize it, but she was his.

He'd fight her every step of the way before she left. He knew it'd be quite a fight, too. Nothing was ever easy with Emma.

They did nothing but hold their position as they stared at one another. Her gaze, although intense, didn't display an ounce of what she was truly thinking. He saw the passion blazing, the need, the want burning in her eyes. But beyond that, he couldn't be sure what she was thinking. It was crazy to hope it was along the same lines as him. That she wasn't leaving. Not for anything.

Her hands tightened on his back.

Wow. He couldn't believe he was having these kind of thoughts while deep inside a woman. He'd never felt like this. Thought such things while having sex.

That was the thing about Emma. She brought out all these new emotions he had never experienced before. How could he let a woman who made him feel this way get away? He couldn't.

Still, with no words, he started to move, slowly, with as much patience as he could muster. He wanted this moment to last as long as possible. He wanted to savor her, enjoy every small movement, every light touch.

She met his slow pace, matching his controlled eagerness.

They moved as one as the pleasure built in the room. In and out. Kisses landed on her neck, his tongue doing things that he couldn't stop even if he tried, as her hands trailed a path up his back, then down to his ass where she would squeeze and play until his movements started to get faster and faster. His lips and tongue continued their assault as their bodies increased the pace, the desire so fierce he was afraid his heart would never survive if she left him.

His thrusts became harder, more intense, as his tongue trailed a path to her ear, where he nibbled lightly. A low moan echoed from her sweet lips.

"Emma..." He cut his whispered words off before he ruined the moment. Because he knew without a doubt she'd run screaming from the room if he begged her not to leave. Something he desperately wanted to do in that moment.

To his disappointment, the moment ended as they both came together in such a frenzy, it almost tore him apart.

Their heavy breathing filled the room as they both came down from the high slowly.

Her arms were tight around his back, his lips still lingering on her neck, peppering light kisses everywhere.

"Well, let's get started on round two."

He lifted his head, laughter floating out. Her eyes sparkled with happy satisfaction. "You got it, sweetheart."

Within that time, he could think of how he'd convince her to stay.

With him.

9

WRITING PROMPT: WHAT WAS THAT SOUND?

Cold air rushed in after him as the door slowly closed. He almost kept walking to the break room, but veered to the front desk instead. It would be odd if he didn't say hi to Daphne, something he did every single time he came into the police station.

As he thought about it, he had come in a lot, sometimes with lame ass excuses to see Aiden when he only wanted to see Daphne. He wanted to slap his hand against his forehead at how transparent he had been about his crush.

But that was in the past.

He'd moved on.

He had Emma now. Whether she knew it or not.

Most likely not.

Last night had been one of the best nights of his life. One of the best nights of sex, for sure. He had tried his damndest to get her to spend the night, but in the end, she stuck to her guns and made him drive her home. She had even threatened to walk by herself—almost did, too, until he pulled her into his arms and wiped that idea clear out of her head with a sultry kiss. She didn't make it home for another thirty minutes after that.

The remaining part of the night had been lonely and quiet. He hated every minute. Barely got a wink of sleep.

Being back to work today made him feel good, otherwise, he probably would've been a grouch from the lack of sleep. He was also grateful the chief changed the schedule the week before Christmas. Instead of working two full twenty-four hour shifts in a row—like they generally did—the chief decided to have everyone rotating on a ten-hour shift. This way everyone had time to spend with their families instead of being stuck at the firehouse. Christmastime was the only time he allowed it.

He couldn't wait for tonight. Emma would be coming over again.

Well, he hoped so. She hadn't actually answered his question about dinner when he asked. But he knew when he fully accepted his feelings for her—which sort of rammed into him like a deer jumping in front of a moving vehicle, quick and unexpected—that it wouldn't be easy for her to see how good they could be together.

Patience.

Lots and lots of patience.

"Hey, Bentley. How was your weekend?"

He couldn't suppress the stupid grin on his face. It had been a damn good weekend. "It was fine. And yours?"

She rolled her eyes, an uncommon gesture for her. "Stressful. Planning a wedding is no easy thing. I have a favor to ask of you." She leaned forward with eager anticipation.

Normally his heart would do a slow pitter-patter of excitement that Daphne wanted anything from him. Instead, he felt a moment of dread.

How would Emma feel about it? Whatever *it* was.

His grin didn't slip, even as he wanted to flee as fast as he could. "Sure. What's up?"

"You know how we're trying to do most of the wedding preparations ourselves instead of hiring people to do it? It's just, we ran into a little snag about setting up the reception hall where we're getting married. My brother Nathan isn't flying in until the night before the wedding," she rolled her eyes, again, an extremely uncommon gesture, "and my dad hurt his arm at work. He can't lift anything heavy for the next few weeks. Would you be able to help set up tables and chairs the night before? I wouldn't ask if I didn't desperately need the help."

Desperately need the help? Since when couldn't Daphne ask him for something? Why did it sound like he was a last resort?

Why the hell did he care if he was?

He had Emma now.

He did.

"Not a problem, Daph. Of course I'll help out."

She swiped a hand over her hair, as if a loose strand had gotten in her way, which it hadn't. Her hair was pulled back into a ponytail without a hair out of place. "Oh, good. That's so good to hear. Thank you so much."

His brows wrinkled as a frown formed. "Is everything okay? I'll always help you."

"Of course. I'm fine. I just...don't want to upset your...Emma."

"Why would it upset her?" Dumb question, of course. He thought the same thing moments before she even asked him. What gave her the impression Emma was his... anything? There's no way she could've known they slept together already.

Her eyes looked down at her desk. "No reason." She then looked at him with a bright smile, as if they didn't just have the weirdest conversation. "She seems nice."

"She is." He tapped the counter lightly as he offered a smile that he had to force. "I should get going, but I'll be there to help."

He turned around after Daphne said goodbye and walked as fast as he could back outside. As soon as the door closed behind him, he realized he never did go talk to Aiden as he originally planned.

Well, hell. He didn't have time now.

He had someone else he needed to speak to. Some answers that needed to be weaseled out.

Because he knew Emma wouldn't make it easy on him when he asked what the hell she said to Daphne. He had no doubt in his mind that's what had to have happened for Daphne to act so weird.

Man, were they about to spar.

SPRINKLES FELL EVERYWHERE as she shook a little harder than was necessary. First, they didn't want to come out. Now, they decided to release like a raging waterfall. Could nothing go right this morning?

She had an awkward breakfast this morning eating with Elliot and Lynn, although neither asked about her night with Bentley. Either because they knew what she did with him, or she had already burned her bridges with two of the nicest people on the planet and they didn't care about her anymore.

Ugh!

She started shaking the sprinkles harder over the

Christmas cookies as that thought burned through her mind.

No matter how hard she tried, she couldn't get the melancholy feeling to dissipate that she wouldn't be welcome in their home much longer with her sour attitude. But she didn't know how to change it.

"Knock, knock."

Her gaze whipped to the swinging door of the bakery to find Bentley smiling, his eyes roaming her body, devouring her with one smooth look.

Just one look and the man had her wanting to pant for more.

What was she going to do about him and the crazy things he made her feel?

"Shouldn't you be at work?"

He shrugged as he moved closer, but still separated by the counter between them. "I am. If they need me, my phone will go off."

"How is your first day back?"

"Uneventful. Which is a good thing." His eyes scanned the table. "Lots of sprinkles going on here."

Rolling her eyes, she avoided his gaze as she doused some more sprinkles on the cookies, even though they didn't need any more. "I'm not much of a baker. Whatever."

A low sigh released. "Is something wrong? Are you..."

She looked up. "Am I what?"

He shrugged again. "Regretting last night or something?"

"It was sex. I never regret sex." She smiled, trying to hide how much she actually enjoyed last night.

It wasn't *just* sex. She had simple sex before, one-night stands that meant nothing. Last night with Bentley...had been everything. The things he made her feel, the closeness, the sweetness in his touch, the tenderness in his words. He made her feel wanted and cared for.

But she couldn't let him know any of that. Because when he broke her heart, which she figured would happen eventually, he'd have weapons at his disposal to hurt her even more.

His eyes narrowed before a chuckle escaped. "Are you coming over for dinner tonight?"

What just happened? It felt like he was about to argue with her about her comment, and then he decided to ignore it. Why?

Well, whatever. She didn't want to talk about it, anyway.

"I guess."

Another chuckle floated between them. "Please, don't sound so excited."

A slow grin emerged as the laughter touched her eyes, yet she didn't make a sound. "It takes a lot to get me excited."

His eyes glittered with instant desire. "I know."

Her insides immediately turned to goo, her heart slamming hard against her chest, her hands trembling from the pleasure in his intense gaze. The man sure knew how to make her melt with one powerful look.

He cleared his throat as his eyes darted away. "So...how do you like Mulberry?"

She instantly went on guard. "Why?"

His gaze gradually connected with hers. "Have you met Daphne yet?"

Oh, boy. Here we go. She was about to get dumped right after he invited her over.

She wouldn't say she said anything mean to the woman this morning when she came in for a box of doughnuts for the precinct, but...she also wasn't overly friendly.

She couldn't stomach the thought Bentley had pined over Daphne for as long as he did. What did he find so special about her? She smiled too much, her hair was too perfect. Little miss perfection.

Well, sorry. Nobody was perfect. Not even Daphne.

So, yeah, she might've been a little brusque and curt with her this morning. But she wanted to pat herself on the back, because she held her tongue. Something extremely hard for her, because she normally said what was on her mind, regardless of the consequences. But for Bentley's sake —plus she didn't want to upset him so soon in their tumultuous relationship—she bit her tongue to refrain from spewing every nasty word in the dictionary at the woman.

"She came in this morning for doughnuts."

"And…how did that go?"

Rolling her eyes, she shook the sprinkles even harder as the rage started to flow. "Is there a point to this lame ass interrogation? Little miss sunshine complaining about me or something?" She kept her eyes trained on him as she kept shaking the sprinkles. "What am I, Bentley? An amusement to get you through the holidays until she's married? A distraction? Because I refuse to be that for you. I might not be as perfect as her, but I have standards. I won't be used."

His eyes glanced down to the tray of cookies before her. "I think that's enough sprinkles."

She followed his gaze and attempted to act nonchalant at the fact she practically poured the entire bottle of sprinkles on one cookie. Jerking at the soft hand on her arm, she looked at Bentley, surprised she never heard him move to her side of the counter.

A warm hand cupped her cheek as a sweet, tender smile graced his face. "I was thinking about making spaghetti tonight. Do you like spaghetti?"

Her eyebrows burrowed as confusion took over. He was really going to ignore everything she just said. She was being serious. Absolutely serious. She would not be played. By anyone. Especially by this handsome, annoying man.

"With garlic toast. I almost forgot to mention that."

She didn't know what to think, and his soft touch was suddenly soothing her rattled nerves. Her anger from moments before deflated as he pressed closer to her.

"I'll even have dessert ready. What's your favorite kind of dessert?"

A hand slid around her waist. The first thing that came to mind popped out. "Whipped cream."

A silky, masculine chuckle filled her bruised, aching heart. "I love whipped cream."

His lips met hers, softly, slowly, and so sweet that she almost begged him to find an empty room to take her hard and fast. She needed to release all the pent up emotions from the last few minutes.

He gradually let go and backed away. She missed him immediately.

"I have to say, you'd win a sprinkling contest. Keep up the good work." He winked and then walked out of the bakery.

She glanced at the cookie filled with sprinkles galore, and then to the door that still swung slightly from his departure.

Did they argue or not?

And why, when he aggravated her more times than not, was she looking forward to tonight?

The damn irritating man was making it hard to resist him. Exceedingly hard.

❄

"HEY, I tried to find you earlier, but then..." Bentley shrugged. "I got distracted."

Aiden nodded as he took a sip of coffee and winced.

Bentley chuckled. "Bad batch today, huh?"

A chuckle floated between them as the cold wind swirled around. "It could be better. I love my wife, though, no matter how horrible her coffee is. What's up?"

Now he felt stupid. Earlier today, when he decided to talk to Aiden about doing something special for Emma, it seemed like a great idea. Now, not so much. He didn't think any ideas Aiden threw out would be good enough. Because Emma was the most difficult person in the world.

He couldn't even get out a simple question. He wanted to ask her what she said to Daphne. A very simple question. So easy.

But the hurt, the ache in her voice when she hollered at him. The things she said...*I might not be as perfect as her, but I have standards.* What made her think she wasn't good enough? What made her think Daphne was perfect? Nobody was perfect.

As soon as those words tore from her mouth, he couldn't ask anything else. He decided to drop the subject and pray she would still join him tonight, which she thankfully was.

Now he couldn't even ask his best friend for help, because he was on shaky ground with her. The littlest thing could set her off.

He'd have to solve this one on his own.

"Bentley? Everything okay?"

He rubbed a gloved hand down his face and groaned. "Yeah, everything's fine."

"Yet you groaned like you're in agony."

"I don't want to screw up this thing with Emma. Daphne asked me to help set up the night before her wedding and..."

He didn't even know how to explain his crazy erratic emotions right now.

"And you don't know how to tell Emma. Because she knows about your little crush you had on Daphne."

"It's not a big deal, right?" Bentley shrugged like it shouldn't be a big deal. He was setting up tables and chairs. Not meeting her for a clandestine evening.

"It shouldn't be. You know women, though." Aiden winced, then chuckled.

"You're a terrible best friend. You are not easing my worries."

His laughter increased in volume. "Dude, you never let up on me when I started dating Theresa. Payback is fair."

A loud boom cracked through the air.

They both flinched.

"What was that sound? That can't be good." Aiden frowned as they both glanced down Main Street past the diner and bakery and to the intersection not too far away.

A shiver rushed down his spine as he saw smoke filter from around the corner. "I think someone just crashed."

His footsteps pounded on the hard cement sidewalk, his heart skipping a beat as he ran toward the smoke, Aiden one step behind him. He could hear Aiden speaking into his radio, asking for medical assistance. By the loud sound that shook the street, he didn't doubt whoever crashed would need medical help.

The sound was so thunderous, people started to exit from the buildings. He even saw Theresa step outside the diner as he and Aiden rushed past. He turned the corner at the end of the street and immediately slid an arm around the guy trying to hobble out of a sporty car that had collided with a mailbox.

"Take it slow and easy. Does anything hurt?"

"My…leg." The man groaned in agony as Bentley helped him sit down on the freezing sidewalk.

"An ambulance is on the way. Hang tight." He stood up and turned to Aiden, whispering, "I can smell alcohol on his breath."

Aiden's expression tensed, his gaze intent and lethal at the man sprawled on the sidewalk moaning in pain. "I'll follow him to the hospital. He won't be leaving my sight."

Bentley nodded, then started to turn back toward the man when a voice to his right made him pause.

"Jared? What are you doing here?"

Bentley glanced at Emma, her eyes round with shock, and if he wasn't mistaken, disgust. "You know this guy, Emma?"

"Of course she knows me. I'm her boyfriend," the man muttered under his breath, then grabbed his leg as another wave of pain must've hit him.

Bentley's eyes narrowed as he glared at the guy, then his gaze connected with Emma's. A slew of emotions hit him. Anger. Irritation. Heartbreak. Intense rage. Yet, no expression could be deciphered in her gaze. Nothing but indifference.

He felt like a fool for falling for her.

A colossal fool.

10

Emma took a seat at the counter, breathing deeply, trying her hardest to keep her cool. The moment Bentley glared at her in disgust and then ignored her while he finished helping Jared until an ambulance arrived couldn't be erased from her mind.

So much disgust.

All because of Jared. The lying, cheating bastard. The sniveling, weak coward.

Another deep breath.

"You look like you could use a drink. A strong drink."

Emma looked at Theresa, who stood on the opposite side of the counter. She didn't even know what possessed her to walk into the diner. After leaving the crash site, she headed to the bakery, where Lynn told her to take the rest of the day off. Lynn was too perceptive. She obviously saw her anger, her rage. The intense rage flowing through her veins.

Yet, she didn't question her. She didn't ask what was wrong. She simply said to enjoy the rest of the day off.

What was there to enjoy? Bentley hated her guts. He didn't even give her the courtesy of letting her explain herself. And by the repulsive glare on his face, he wasn't planning to.

"Are you okay, Emma?"

Shrugging, she wished she had a strong drink in front of her.

"I get off in twenty minutes. Do you want to get a drink?"

The kindness in Theresa's eyes almost overwhelmed her. True, honest to goodness, kindness. Nothing like Ashley, her supposed best friend.

"I think I'd like that."

Theresa smiled. "Great. Why don't I grab you a coffee while you wait?"

Emma nodded. Maybe keeping her hands wrapped around a coffee mug, instead of clenched into tight fists, would help calm her rage. Theresa set a steaming hot mug in front of her and then walked away to help another customer.

The first sip almost made her choke as the coffee slid down her throat with unease. A bitter taste coated her mouth as she debated whether to take another sip. Would Theresa be offended if she didn't drink any more?

Boy, Aiden hadn't lied when he said his wife made terrible coffee.

A slow bubble of laughter slipped out. Before she could hide her amusement, Theresa glanced at her a few feet away.

"I know. It's a terrible pot today." Theresa started to giggle.

It wasn't that funny, but Emma started to laugh harder. Glancing around, she saw a few other patrons giggling as well.

Like that, the rage consuming her slowly ebbed away until only a mild madness lingered. It probably would until she could either ream Jared out for uttering what he did, or give Bentley a piece of her mind for his judgmental behavior.

Thirty minutes later, she and Theresa were seated at the counter of the local bar with two shot glasses in front of them. They both downed their shots. A fruity flavor, with a hint of a nasty taste, coated her throat as it slid down until it settled in her stomach.

Already her body started to relax, a smooth mellow feeling coming over her.

"So, do you want to talk about it?"

Emma wasn't much of a talker, even with the few close friends she'd had in high school. Ashley had been her best friend, until she suddenly wasn't. Until she realized everything she had ever confided to Ashley had been the worst decision ever.

"It's okay if you don't want to. I understand."

Emma glanced at Theresa. She had no doubt Theresa did understand and that she wasn't just giving her a bunch of words.

"That guy...who crashed. He's my ex boyfriend." She rolled her eyes. "I don't even know how he found me. Or why."

Theresa rubbed the side of the glass of the fruity drink she ordered before they downed the shots. "It sounded like he thinks you're still dating."

"Yeah, apparently." Emma suddenly wished for another shot, besides the beer she had ordered. She lifted her finger to the bartender. "But we're not. I don't waste my time on cheaters."

Theresa winced, then took a sip of her drink. "What an asshole."

Emma chuckled. "You have no idea."

The bartender smiled as he stopped in front of them. "What can I get ya?"

"I'll take another shot, please."

He nodded as he grabbed the ingredients to make another Red Headed Slut shot for her. "Do you want another one, too, Theresa?"

They looked at each other, then Theresa nodded. "I'd love another one, Stu."

He made the drinks quickly and then filled their shot glasses up. They clinked glasses before downing the shots.

Emma winced as the nasty flavor mixed with the fruitiness slid down her throat, but she couldn't stop the giggle. "This drink is so fitting. The name of it…" Emma started to laugh harder.

Theresa joined in on the laughter, even though she had no clue why Emma was laughing so hard.

Why not share it all?

"My best friend Ashley, a red head, slept with that asshole." Emma laughed so hard, she snorted.

Theresa's mouth widened in shock. "That…slut."

Another round of giggles erupted between the two.

It felt wonderful to let loose. To laugh as if she didn't have a care in the world. And in that moment, she didn't.

She found a new friend.

The thought of leaving made her even sadder. Because then she wouldn't have Theresa in her life anymore. Or Lynn. Or Elliot. Leaving wouldn't be sad because of Bentley, the annoying, irritating man that she couldn't help but adore, but she would be miserable leaving everyone else behind, too.

Stu stopped in front of them, a sweet grin on his face. "Having fun, ladies?"

"Hell yeah, Stu. Give us another round." Emma waved her hands at the shot glasses.

Stu eyed Theresa, waiting for her approval. When she nodded with enthusiasm, he filled the glasses up again.

Emma raised her shot glass. "Thanks, Theresa. I needed this."

Theresa lightly tapped her glass. "That's what real friends are for."

A strange emotion hit her chest as another shot washed down her throat, the nasty flavor oddly getting easier to stomach with the more shots she took. The mellow feeling from before intensified.

Real friends.

Yeah, she would love to call Theresa a real friend. It felt nice.

She never wanted to leave this small town.

"HEY, man. What are you still doing here?"

Bentley looked up into Aiden's worried eyes. He sat in a chair in the hospital waiting area, just sitting. Trying to forget the look of heartbreak on Emma's face when he walked away.

God, he was such an idiot.

He didn't say anything or give her a chance to explain herself.

Such an idiot.

He stood up. "I was curious about that guy. Are you charging him with anything?"

"Oh, yeah. DUI, for sure. He blew a .12. He's sitting nicely in a room with his hand cuffed to the bed and his leg in a cast." Aiden blew out a breath. "Have you talked to Emma yet?"

He averted his gaze. "No. I'm a little worried about how mad she is at me."

"Mad at you? That dude said he was her boyfriend. Shouldn't you be mad at her?"

"I should at least give her the courtesy of explaining things to me. The guy *is* drunk. Maybe he isn't her boyfriend."

"I didn't hear her dispute it."

"You're not helping me right now, Aiden." He chuckled, even though nothing was funny.

Aiden shrugged as his grin grew, the worry still coating his eyes. "I hope it was just the ramblings of a drunk guy."

"Me, too." *You have no idea.*

A peppy Christmas song filled the room. Bentley looked at Aiden funny as he laughed, pulling out his phone. "Theresa set the ring tone." He looked at the screen. "Give me a moment."

More time to himself. Something he didn't want. He should've tracked Emma down right away after he took care of the vehicle, getting it off the street and to the mechanics.

She could call him a coward, or a multitude of other names. He wouldn't be surprised if she let loose with every vile name in the book at him. That's how spirited she could be, how lively, how honest she was.

He loved that about her.

"So, yeah, I think we should go."

Bentley met Aiden's gaze and watched as he slid his phone back onto his belt. "Is there a problem?"

A deep, throaty laugh spilled out. "Well, if you call Theresa and Emma getting so drunk Stu called me to come get them, then yeah, we have a problem."

"Drunk? Are you serious?" Bentley followed him outside.

"I guess they're having a grand time taking shots, laughing the joint up, and...having fun."

"Are they being too loud? Are they..."

"No, Stu said they aren't disrupting the place, but Theresa doesn't generally drink that much. You know, she's trying to help support her brother James in a sense, by toning down her drinking. Stu just thought he'd give me a call." Aiden paused. "He did say Emma was taking a lot more shots than Theresa. He was a little concerned about her."

So was he. So much so, his heart started to race, his hands shook, and his legs felt like Jello as he slid into his truck. He couldn't get to the bar fast enough. He couldn't even explain why he was so worried about her. She was a big girl. She didn't need him to watch out for her or worry about her.

He did anyway.

He followed Aiden to the bar, although had been sorely tempted to pass him and speed the entire way. Aiden must not be too concerned, because he took his time driving. By the time Bentley parked, his heart was pounding so badly he was afraid it'd jump right out of his chest.

The minute Aiden pulled open the door and he stepped through after him, his heart calmed a fraction at hearing Emma's sweet laughter.

"Aiden, honey. You're here. How awesome is that? Isn't that awesome?" Theresa launched herself into his arms. Aiden chuckled and wrapped his arms tight around his wife as she started to shower him with kisses.

Bentley's gaze connected with Emma's. Her eyes sparkled with laughter and a bit of mischief. A sweet but sexy grin adorned her exquisite face. He approached her slowly, praying she wouldn't be able to hear the pounding of his heart.

"Hello, pookey bear." She laughed as she patted his cheek. "You look so dashing right now."

Oh, she was drunk alright. Pookey bear? Dashing? He was wearing jeans and a large winter coat. He wouldn't exactly call that dashing.

"Sounds like you're having fun."

"We're having a blast. Stuey, grab us some shots," Emma hollered, waving to Stu, who stood at the other end of the bar helping another patron. He smiled and nodded, but then turned back to the other customer.

"Yay, more shots." Theresa high-fived Emma, then launched herself into Aiden's arms again.

"Yeah, I think no more shots tonight, sweetheart. You are going to have a helluva hangover tomorrow." Aiden tightened his grip when Theresa tried to sit back down.

"But we're having soooooo much fun," Theresa whined. Then she kissed him on the lips. "Where's a mistletoe when I need one?"

Aiden chuckled. "You don't need a mistletoe to kiss me." He demonstrated by kissing her soundly on the lips. Then Aiden looked up and his eyes connected with Bentley's, communicating with one glance that he was taking his wife home.

He nodded.

"You're such a party pooper, Aiden." Emma had a grin on her face, but Bentley heard the tone in her voice. She might be drunk, but she wasn't happy Aiden was taking her drinking partner away.

"You'll both thank me tomorrow when your headache isn't as bad as it could be." He smiled, then ushered Theresa out of the building, but not before Theresa grabbed a hug from Emma and insisted they do this again.

"I'll give you a ride home."

Emma turned away. "I ordered another shot." She patted the empty seat next to her. "Sit down, pookey bear."

Bentley glanced at Stu, who still stood at the other end of the bar, most likely taking his time on purpose.

He moved closer to her, but didn't sit down. Leaning near her ear, he whispered, "Come, my lady. Let pookey bear take you home."

A shiver ran down her spine as she turned to meet his gaze. His lips were precariously close to hers, yet he didn't kiss her. He could smell the alcohol on her breath. She was wasted. He didn't want her to regret anything, and being this drunk, she might the next morning.

Was that guy really her boyfriend? He needed that answered, too, before he kissed her again.

A sexy smile touched her lips. "Okay. You can take me home." She stood up, wobbling into his arms. "Your home. My new home."

His arms tightened around her waist as his heart started to jump like mad again.

Her head fell to his chest. "I never want to leave. Don't make me leave, Bentley."

His breath hitched. Did she know what she was saying?

Because he never wanted her to leave. Ever.

"We'll take the check, Stu." He grabbed for his wallet without letting her go and tossed his card on the counter.

"You feel so soft." She snuggled into his embrace. "Like a big teddy bear."

He chuckled as he rubbed a hand up and down her back. "Don't worry, pookey bear is going to take care of you."

"Always?" She wrapped her arms tighter around him.

"Promise me for always? I couldn't bear if another person that I loved left me. They always leave me."

Love?

Did she just say she loved him?

Oh, boy.

If his heart hadn't fallen for her days ago, he definitely would've in this moment.

Her sad, broken words pained him. Gutted him straight to the core. She sounded so lost and dejected, he wanted to make her world a brighter and happier place. No matter what he had to do to achieve that.

He'd do anything for her.

He bent his head and kissed her neck. "I'll never leave you. As long as you promise not to leave me."

A light snore answered him.

Leaning back slightly, he couldn't hold the chuckle in when he saw her eyes were closed. She confessed she loved him, then promptly fell asleep.

Wow.

And he still didn't know if that guy was her boyfriend.

But she loved him.

He could live with that. The other guy didn't matter.

Because she loved him.

11

A loud pounding hammered in her ear. She grabbed the pillow underneath her head and smothered her face to drown out the noise.

"Make it stop. Stop pounding on the door."

The pillow disappeared, then a warm hand brushed across her forehead. Her eyes slowly opened and met Bentley's tender stare.

"Who's at the door?"

His smile pricked her heart as he slowly sat down next to her on the bed, setting the pillow near her head. Her mind started to race as she tried to remember how she got in his bed.

"No one is at the door. I imagine that's your head pounding like crazy." His sweet, yet sexy smile grew.

Her eyes closed as his words started to register, the pounding increasing like a bunch of mad men trying to break down a door. "I had a lot to drink last night, didn't I?"

"Oh, just a little." His hand touched her shoulder. "Come on, open your eyes. Drink up."

When she opened her eyes, the bright light hit her like a

two-by-four smacking her between the shoulder blades. She wanted to close them again so badly, but her gaze caught the glass of water in his hands.

Still with that sweet, gentle smile of his, he handed her two white pills and the water. She sat up slightly, downing the pills and water eagerly, then laid back down, closing her eyes as soon as her head hit the bed.

She attempted to sift through her memories from last night, coming up blank. The last time she drank this much was Ashley's twenty-first birthday and they closed the joint down, almost risking the cops getting called when they refused to leave. They met some guys that night and...yeah, it was quite a night. She still couldn't remember most of it.

Or about last night.

"So..."

A low, masculine chuckle rented the air. "Yep."

"Yep, what?" She couldn't open her eyes to see the confirmation that she acted like a fool last night. Or was he saying yep for another reason? What did yep mean?

"Yep, you're beautiful and funny and so damn adorable when you're drunk."

She cracked her eyes open, almost laughing at the charming sparkle in his gaze. He meant what he said. That gave her hope she didn't say or do anything too crazy. "So...I wasn't a complete idiot last night?"

His eyes glittered with intensity. Of what, she couldn't be sure. Desire? Regret? She didn't like not being able to decipher his look.

"I don't think it was too bad. I'm sure Stuey would agree."

A giggle escaped. "Who is Stuey?"

Bentley joined in the laughter. "The bartender. His name is Stu. By the time I got there with Aiden, you were calling him Stuey and asking for more shots. I'm sure Theresa has a pounding headache, just like you."

She closed her eyes again as she laid a hand over her forehead. A smile still touched her lips. "I had fun. It's been a long time since I had fun like that." The confession slipped out before she could stop herself. "I haven't..." She couldn't confess any more.

A warm hand landed on her waist. "We should talk, but we can do it later. I know your head hurts."

Or she could confess now. She hated talking, expressing her feelings, but with Bentley—she felt compelled to. As if she didn't, she might lose him for good, and she wasn't ready to lose him. Not yet. She just found him.

"I haven't had a good time in a long time because my best friend slept with my boyfriend. The jackass from yesterday." She moved her hand away from her forehead as she looked at Bentley. "He isn't my boyfriend anymore, and he hasn't been for the past few months."

"Do you know why he's here?"

Her hand found his that rested on her waist. Their fingers intertwined. "No clue. I don't want to see him again."

"Then you won't."

The fierce intent in his eyes made her instantly believe him. If she wanted Jared to leave her alone, Bentley would take care of it. She had no doubt in her mind.

Her heart started to pound in tune with her aching headache.

She couldn't let Bentley take care of her problems.

His expression didn't waver. The intensity, the determination in his gaze made her shiver.

With anticipation.

For the first time, in the longest time, she had hope her future could be a happy one.

Her eyes drifted closed once again.

A light kiss touched her cheek. "I did something crazy."

With that confession, her eyes popped open. Bentley's lips were a breath away, his gaze strong and…passionate?

"I feel like I should be worried."

His lips curled into a devilish grin. "You should be."

"What did you do?"

His lips came closer. "I called out sick for you…and me."

That wasn't so crazy. She had called out before after a night of too much drinking.

Then his lips connected with hers briefly.

Well, maybe it was a bit crazy. She knew exactly how they'd be spending the day.

And she wouldn't change anything. That was the craziest thing of all.

She closed her eyes, needing a bit more sleep before she would be able to function properly. A light kiss hit her cheek as the blankets were pulled up around her and she was snuggled underneath like a child being tucked in. A sweet smile touched her lips at how thoughtful he was being. She liked being taken care of.

She promptly fell asleep, waking a few hours later. A warm arm was draped across her stomach, her body cocooned with Bentley's. A gentle smile touched her lips as she laid a hand over his.

A kiss hit her shoulder. "Good morning…again. How's your head feeling?"

"Much better."

His embrace tightened as another kiss touched her shoulder. "What do you want to do today? I don't normally call out like this, especially…"

She stilled, a strange tension filling her more quickly than she liked. "Especially, what?"

His hot breath slid down her spine as his mouth got closer to her neck. "Especially since I recently got reamed by my boss. He's not exactly happy with me." He nibbled on her ear. "And I don't particularly care right now."

Her grin widened as she turned around in his arms, then brightened even more when she saw the desire sparkling in his eyes. "So you're all mine all day?"

"And all night."

He bent his head to kiss her when she put a finger to his lips. "Hold that thought. I need to brush my teeth. I feel disgusting."

"You're beautiful. And you won't be hearing me say otherwise." He swatted her ass playfully after she rolled out of bed giggling. "There's an extra toothbrush underneath the sink."

She found the toothbrush, slabbed a healthy dose of toothpaste on the brush, and brushed her teeth quickly. Practically jumping back in bed, causing him to laugh with her, she resumed the same position from before she left the bed.

"You may now continue your sweet, sweet kiss."

"About damn time. You took forever, my lady," he whispered softly before claiming her lips.

The kiss was slow and sensual, gradually building until she wanted to feel him skin to skin. It wasn't difficult to get to that point, as he was already half naked. She tugged on his boxers to signal what she wanted. A grin punctured his face against her lips, then he lifted to remove his boxers as she tossed off her shirt and panties.

His lips met hers once again, the heat, the magic building between them like a raging fire catching quickly on a dry field. His hands touched her everywhere. In her hair, smoothing back some stray strands. Down her arm, his fingers skimming her skin, making her shiver in delight. On her hips, his fingers teasing for more to come.

She loved his touch. Anywhere and everywhere.

His lips left hers, making a trail down her chin, to her neck, and up to her ear.

"You are staying tonight."

A tremble coated her body at his soft words. It wasn't quite a question, more like a demand, but she heard the hesitancy in his tone, as if he were unsure of himself.

"Try prying me away."

A chuckle tickled her ear, then a kiss followed. He shifted to his side of the bed, grabbed a condom lying on the nightstand, and entered her a few seconds later. He stilled for a moment, as if savoring how wonderful she felt. Oh, and she couldn't deny how glorious it felt with him inside her. It's as if he was made for her. His body molding to hers. His heartbeat matching the erratic pace of hers.

This, whatever this was between them, she knew without even asking, it was a mutual feeling. Crazy and chaotic, yet perfectly right. He mellowed out her fickle emotions.

With slow patience, he started moving in and out. She grabbed him tightly, her lips pressing to his neck as the passion grew. He loved her with a beauty she had never experienced before. As if he was telling her how he felt without saying the words.

I couldn't bear if another person that I loved left me.

That popped into her head without warning. Her hands on his back tightened.

Did she say that last night?

Did she confess she loved him?

Or did she think this, wanting to confess it?

Because it was true. She wouldn't be able to handle it if

another person she loved left her. She was already as broken as she could possibly be. One more break, and she'd never survive.

He couldn't leave her.

"I won't. I promise."

She shivered at his whispered words that melted her senses as his hot breath rushed down her spine.

Did she say that out loud? She hadn't meant to.

His lips touched her neck as he increased the pace. "You're mine, Emma. All mine. I won't leave you." His thrusts intensified. "Promise me you'll do the same. Don't leave me."

She matched his pace, the ecstasy building to such epic proportions she knew her body would tingle from the aftermath all day.

Yet, she didn't respond.

She didn't know how to respond.

She wanted to promise him. She wanted to confess every strangled emotion she held inside.

But nothing. She couldn't do it.

He jerked two more times, then tensed as his orgasm hit, touching her at the same time. The feeling spread throughout her body, relaxing her, showing her how beautiful love could be.

Another kiss hit her neck. "It's okay, Emma. Sometimes you don't need words to express how you feel."

Her arms tightened around him.

That said it all.

"I don't know if I should do this."

Bentley watched as Aiden rubbed the back of his neck,

wondering why he was so concerned. "I'm not going to kill the man. I want to talk to him."

Aiden's eyes narrowed. "He's still in custody, even though he's in the hospital. That's why I don't think I should do this." He sighed heavily. "Not because I think you'll hurt him."

"Well, I do want to hurt him." Bentley laughed as Aiden's gaze turned stern.

"He lied. He's not her boyfriend anymore, but I don't think that's a good enough reason to talk to him."

"Look, Aiden, I'm going in that room, whether you like it or not. Emma doesn't want him bothering her, and I'm going to make sure he understands that. Why is he here? Did you ask him that?"

Aiden rubbed the back of his neck again. "He hasn't exactly been the most cooperative."

"Five minutes, man. That's all I'm asking."

"If Chief Duncan finds out I let you in this room..." Aiden blew out a breath. "Be quick about it."

Bentley nodded, then stepped around Aiden and opened the door to Jared's room. His leg was wrapped in a white cast, propped up. Jared's eyes darted warily at him as he approached the bed.

"I want out of here."

Bentley glanced around the room, a slow smile forming. "This place is a lot more comfortable than a cell." His eyes landed on his. "I wouldn't be so eager to leave."

"I didn't do anything."

"The mailbox would probably disagree with you."

"You were there. You know Emma." Jared's eyes slid into tiny little slits. "How?"

Bentley leaned closer, his smile dying as the most evil sneer he owned replaced it. "If, and that's a big if, you get released, you'll stay the hell away from her. She doesn't want anything to do with you."

"She's my—"

"Nothing. She's your nothing. She became nothing to you when you slept with her friend."

Jared's gaze fell to his lap. "That was a mistake. I'm trying to fix that mistake."

"If you come within a hundred feet of her, you'll regret it."

Jared jerked his eyes back to him. "Did you seriously threaten me? I'll have your badge."

Bentley leaned even closer, his hands tight into fists. "I'm not a cop. And I don't threaten. I'm telling you the truth. You're not welcome in this town." He would be sure Jared understood that. He'd be sure to tell the one person who could spread things around town as fast as a wildfire burning a dry forest.

Daphne.

Although, confessing why he wanted her to do this for him would be awkward. But for Emma, he'd do it.

"You don't scare me."

A chuckle let loose as he backed away. "Maybe not. But I'm sure Emma does. Do you honestly think she's going to want you back after what you did? If I were you, I'd be very worried about my crown jewels."

Jared's hand instinctively started to reach for the most sensitive spot on his body, but stopped before he reached it. "Who are you?"

"Remember what I said, Jared. As soon as you make bail, if you even do, your ass better be out of this town." He headed for the door, turning toward him before opening it. "Trust me. This town bands together. And you're not going to be getting a welcoming committee."

"Emma's not from here. They don't care about her."

"You're as dumb as you look." He gave Jared the best glare he owned and walked out of the room.

He wasn't about to feed Jared any information about him. What Emma meant to him. The fact that he cared about her, that Chief Duncan cared about her, meant she was a part of this town. Nothing more needed to be said or done. It was that simple. Now, he needed to let Daphne know to spread the word Jared wasn't welcome so everyone in this town knew.

"Well?" Aiden asked as the door closed behind him.

"I didn't even touch him." He patted his shoulder and headed for the exit.

"Where are you going?"

"To talk to Daphne, then to visit my...Emma." He almost said girlfriend. He thought of her as that. He thought Emma probably thought that, too. But they hadn't defined anything.

Yesterday had been a great day. They didn't do anything but have fun in bed and relax in front of the TV, binge-watching shows. This morning, he dropped her off at Elliot's, waiting patiently while she took a quick shower, and then drove her to the bakery and delivered one of the sweetest kisses yet, with promises for more later tonight.

So, yeah. He definitely thought of her as his girlfriend. But honestly, they hadn't known each other that long. One minute they were snapping at each other, the next they were devouring each other. Odd, yet so right.

He wouldn't change a thing.

Aiden's laughter drowned out as he turned the corner. He made it to the precinct a few minutes later, his nerves suddenly emerging with force.

This was no big deal. Him and Daphne were friends.

They had been for a long time. Just because he had a crush on her didn't mean he couldn't talk to her about Emma. His girlfriend.

Yes, his girlfriend.

The more it circled his mind, the better it sounded. He might even try it out tonight to see her reaction.

"Hey, Bentley. How was your day off yesterday?"

He smiled, chuckling at how much Daphne knew. When something happened, she magically knew right away. It could be annoying sometimes. This wasn't one of those times. "It was perfect. Emma and I had a relaxing day."

A sweet smile graced her exquisite face. Not as gorgeous as Emma's, of course. "That's good to hear. I was worried when I heard you called out. I'm glad it wasn't for anything serious. Is Emma okay?"

It shouldn't have surprised him, but it did. Daphne's concern wasn't fake. She honestly wanted to know if Emma was alright. This was just one display of how sweet and kind Daphne could be. The only thing to surprise him was her odd behavior from the weekend, which, thankfully, was gone.

"She's fine. Thanks for asking." He leaned against the counter between them. "So, the guy in the hospital..."

He proceeded to feed Daphne information that would have everyone hating the man on sight, which wouldn't be too difficult. He did drive into town, drunk, and crash into a mailbox, unconcerned about the damage he might cause.

What he didn't do was go into detail about the pain he caused Emma. That wasn't Daphne's, or anyone else's, business unless Emma wanted them to know.

The mischievous smile on Daphne's face told him everything he needed to know.

She would do her thing, and Jared would never show his face in town again after he was released from custody.

Emma would be safe. Jared couldn't hurt her anymore.

Her happiness was his top priority.

He needed to buy her a Christmas present. That thought popped into his head as he stepped outside into the blistering cold.

And not just any Christmas present. But the best one out there.

He just didn't know what that was yet.

12

"Have a great day, Mrs. Wayworth," Emma said with a smile, waving as Mrs. Wayworth walked out of the bakery with a box of Christmas cookies decorated with the sweetest icing she had ever tasted.

Lynn was a bakery goddess.

She swore her smile was frozen on her face with all the smiling she had been performing today. Customer after customer bustling through the door for baked goodies, preparing for holiday parties or simply wanting something delicious to eat.

They all came to Lynn's.

She honestly wasn't surprised. She would start getting fat if she didn't stop eating half the stuff Lynn baked.

Everyone was so nice. Not like the town she grew up in.

Well, okay. Most people were nice, but growing up as the chief's daughter hadn't always been easy. She had to be on her best behavior. The perfect child. As a young girl, she had been awkward and shy.

Then her teen years hit. Her dad was always working.

Work, work, work. Slowly, the rebellion in her grew and grew until she couldn't control it anymore.

Analyzing her own behavior, she knew why. She wanted a little of her father's attention. She wouldn't say he had been a terrible father, he just worked too much. He was always so concerned about the people in town, keeping them safe, she fell to the wayside more times than not.

When Elliot showed up when she was ten years old, it had been one of the best years of her life. He had been there for an internship from the local college in St. Cloud. Robertsville, being the closest small town, had been his choice to intern under her father for his senior year.

Her dad, being the friendly, open man he was, treated Elliot not like another intern, or even an officer, but a member of the family. As he did with all his employees. For whatever reason, Elliot took that to heart. He treated her like an uncle, or an older brother, unlike some of the other employees her father had.

She clung to him, hung on his every word, worshiped him. He had been the uncle she never had. He never treated her like she was a nuisance. Not once.

And then he left.

Life went back to being boring and normal. Where her dad worked too much and rarely had time for her.

Each year, her rebellious nature emerged more and more, and before she knew it, she was roaming from dead end job to dead end job, skipping college, and having no sense of where her future was headed.

But maybe...

No. She shouldn't rely on Bentley. She shouldn't assume just because they had been having such a wonderful time the past few days that it would last.

Nothing ever lasted in her life.

"Hey, I—"

She jumped and screamed as a hand landed on her shoulder. Turning slightly, she started laughing with Lynn, who looked apologetic for scaring her. She couldn't believe she was scared so easily. How silly.

Placing a hand over her racing heart, she waited to speak until her laughter died down. "I'm sorry for screaming. You startled me, obviously."

A gentle smile graced Lynn's face. Her motherly smile. That's what Emma thought every time she saw it, and she loved to display it a lot. Totally crazy, because she wasn't that much younger than Lynn. Only by a few years. "It's okay. I didn't mean to surprise you. How was Mrs. Wayworth? Her sister is due in a month."

A warmth of pleasure spread through her. It touched her that Lynn assumed Mrs. Wayworth shared personal, joyful information with her. Like she was a part of this town or something.

Something she desperately wanted.

"Well, she couldn't stop raving about your cookies, actually ate one before she left. And she talked up Theresa's jewelry, which she tells me I need to own something made by her."

Lynn's eyes brightened. "You do. She makes wonderful jewelry."

"Her sister is doing well. I think they're worried about her blood pressure, though. She has an induction set for three weeks from now."

Lynn's gaze turned worried. "I'll call her later. See if she needs anything. I hope it all goes well."

She watched as Lynn placed a protective hand over her large belly. "I'm sure it'll all be fine."

"Will you be joining us for supper tonight?"

Her expression froze. She had planned to spend the evening with Bentley again. She missed him. Someone who had barely been in her life for less than a few weeks, and she missed him as if she had known him her entire life.

But Elliot was an important part of her life. One of the most important parts. She could finally admit it. Why else did she put a box together and claim her father wanted him to have it? When really, she needed an excuse to see him. To cling to a small part of her old life that was slowly disappearing.

She needed to express her regret to Lynn somehow. Bentley should've never had to call out for her when Lynn needed the help. She was a terrible employee. Selfish.

This new life scared her. It frightened her so much, she wanted to curl up and cry. Shed all the tears she couldn't shed when her dad died.

With her dad gone, even though he worked all the time, she now had no one.

All alone in the world.

A warm hand touched her shoulder. This time she didn't flinch. "Why don't you and Bentley join us for supper?"

She connected eyes with her. "Elliot might not—"

"Listen to me." Lynn cut her off, yet waited for her to acknowledge she was ready to hear what she wanted to say. Something important, she could tell by the glittered concern in her eyes.

She nodded.

"I'm sorry about your dad." Lynn held up her hand when she opened her mouth to speak. "I can see Elliot's almost like a father figure to you. He does love you like you're family. I care about you, too. Now, I know Bentley. As does Elliot. He's a wonderful man. I won't dispute that." The hand on her shoulder tightened in comfort. "But I think it would be good to let Elliot play his role. Let Bentley know in no uncertain terms that he treats you right. He can do that with one stern gaze over supper." A bright, beautiful smile filled Lynn's face.

Her dad never vetted any of her boyfriends. She went through men so fast, he had no chance to even attempt it. Not to mention, not many wanted to meet the chief of police, so she didn't bring them around the house.

Elliot was the chief of police.

He was like a father figure.

Would Bentley feel comfortable enough to come over?

After Elliot let her in his home, she felt bad for not being around lately. That was rude of her.

But she wanted to be with Bentley. She wanted something between them to work out. Somehow. She didn't know how it'd work out in the long run.

Unless she stayed in town.

"Emma?"

She returned Lynn's smile. "Yeah, okay."

This might be the most awkward supper ever.

She was bringing home a guy to meet *the parents.*

BENTLEY TRIED NOT to fidget or betray the shake in his hands as he unzipped his coat and handed it to Chief Duncan.

He wasn't exactly sure why his nerves were running rampant through his veins like a rogue train going a hundred miles an hour. Chief Duncan already gave him the speech to treat her right.

He sensed he had another one coming his way.

Chief Duncan laid a hand on his shoulder and squeezed lightly. "Relax, Bentley. We had our little chat."

His eyes narrowed slightly. "Unless we need to have another one."

"We're good, Chief."

His eyes twinkled with relief and then he dropped his hand. "Call me, Elliot. Chief Duncan sounds too formal. We're all fa—riends here."

He was going to say family.

Well, it wasn't a surprise to him that Chief Duncan—Elliot—saw Emma as family. But if he ended up, let's say, marrying her, that would make him family.

Odd.

Yet it felt right.

"Come on. Supper is almost ready."

He followed Chief Du—Elliot—into the living room where Emma and Laura sat on the couch watching Frosty the Snowman on the TV.

Emma beamed a sweet, yet sultry smile as their eyes connected. She stood up, almost like she was going to fling herself into his arms, but stopped short when she saw Chief —Elliot—looking at both of them.

He asked him to call him Elliot, but it might take him a while to think of him like that. He always called him Chief Duncan. Because he was the chief. He was a man in a position of authority. It's not like they sat down together and had beers like they were friends or anything. Even Aiden called him Chief Duncan, and he had had beers with him on occasion.

"Don't be shy on my account." Chief—Elliot—chuckled, winked at Laura, who giggled, and then walked out of the room.

"I think Dad meant you could kiss her if you want, Bentley," Laura said with a giggle, her hand covering her mouth.

He smiled. "Thank you for the clarification, Pipsqueak."

"Only Aiden calls me that."

"So that means I can't?" he asked with a teasing tone.

Her eyes turned down as a low shade of red flooded her face. "Maybe."

Lynn had the sweetest little girl. He knew, as well as Aiden, that she had a crush on Aiden. She always turned beet red when he called her pipsqueak. He treated her like his little niece, always making her feel a little extra special. Bentley always treated her the same. He was a little surprised he was being denied use of the nickname.

But he could live with it.

"I can leave the room, too, so you can kiss her properly." Laura giggled again, her eyes darting between them.

"And what do you know about kissing, little missy?" Emma asked.

Bentley's heart started to race at finally hearing her delicate, soft voice. The littlest things could get his heart pumping. He didn't know what he'd do when she lef—

No. He would make sure she didn't want to leave.

He had high hopes she wasn't planning to.

"Nothing." Laura looked away as her cheeks burned a bright red again.

Emma laughed, pointing to herself, then at Laura. "You and me are going to have girl talk later."

"Okay." Laura giggled one more time and then left the room.

As soon as they were alone, Emma launched herself into his arms. He didn't hesitate to claim her lips, dipping his tongue in, savoring her delicious taste, the way she fit so perfectly in his arms.

The kiss eventually slowed until he finally pulled away before he was tempted to search for an empty room to show her how much he truly missed her.

"This is probably going to be the most awkward supper ever."

He grinned. "I don't think so."

"How can you say that? Didn't you see the way Elliot looked at us?"

"Like he's happy to see us happy? I did."

Emma arched a brow with a worried expression touching her lips. "I'm not so sure."

Her apprehension made his heart pound a little faster. It's as if she were trying to create a problem. Like she wanted to distance herself from him.

His hands tightened on her waist.

"He already had the don't-hurt-her-or-I'll-hurt-you speech with me. What's going on? Talk to me."

Surprise flashed across her face. "When did this happen? Why would he do that?"

"He cares about you. He's only looking out for you."

"He's not my father."

Bentley jerked by the venom in her tone, but he didn't let go of her. "What's wrong?"

She tensed, then rested her head against his chest. "Nothing. I'm fine."

His instincts said she wasn't, but he didn't think this was the best time to argue with her, especially with Lynn and Elliot in the other room.

"You know you can tell me anything."

Her hands fisted his shirt. "I said I was fine."

Their relationship felt like a damn ping-pong ball. Back and forth. Back and forth. Bouncing around the table until it suddenly flew off in a direction he didn't expect.

He didn't know what to do but go with the flow and hope she decided to confide in him.

❄

A SOFT KNOCK sounded on the door.

Emma turned slightly, pausing as she packed the small suitcase she had brought with her. Elliot gazed at her with a gentle smile. A friendly one. But definitely with concern mixed in.

She still couldn't get over that he had the speech with Bentley, and that Bentley didn't tell her about it. What did they talk about? Why did Elliot feel compelled to do it? It's not like her and Bentley were that serious.

Then why are you packing your bags and staying with him the duration of your stay?

Wiping that question out of her mind, deciding it was better to ignore it, she flashed him a fake smile and went back to tossing her clothes in the suitcase.

The silence in the room started to crawl up her skin, invading her nerves like ants invading a dirt mound. Yet, she didn't say a word. She honestly didn't know what to say. Elliot offered her a place to stay, he welcomed her into his home, and she felt like she was abandoning him over a guy.

How dumb was that?

She could admit it was pretty dumb.

A warm hand clamped over hers that was stuffing a large white sweater into her suitcase. "We should talk."

"I get it. You hate me now."

He let go of her hand and touched her chin, forcing her to look at him. Concern glittered in his gaze. "Why would I hate you? You and Bentley have a connection. I can relate to that. When I met Lynn..." His hand dropped as a sweet smile punctured his face. "She was like an angel from heaven. She filled up my broken heart with ease. I fell hard, and I fell for her really easily."

"She's great. You're incredibly lucky."

"So are you. He's a good man. And I'm here for you if he doesn't treat you right."

Her eyes trailed to the ground. Hearing those words cut her deeply.

Because they were words she always wanted to hear from her dad. Not that she ever dated the kind of man she wanted her dad to say that about. But he never inquired about her boyfriends, her dates. Hell, he rarely asked about her friends.

He didn't even talk to her about his illness.

He lied over and over again, acting as if nothing was wrong, when nothing was ever going to work out right.

A tear slipped out.

A pair of arms wrapped her into a tight embrace.

More tears came out.

She cried.

She cried all the tears she never cried when her dad died.

Elliot's arms held her tightly through it all. His hand wove up and down her back, soothing, as a father would comfort a child. Her tears intensified.

She never had moments like this with her father. Not even when her mom died when she was six.

That was about the time her dad slowly started to change.

She understood the change, his reasoning for wanting to keep the town safe.

Because he failed at keeping his own wife safe.

She had been leaving the grocery store, not too late in the evening, when two men demanded the keys to her car. She immediately complied and backed away from the vehicle, her groceries all tucked nicely in the back seat.

It should've never happened. It should've been a simple armed carjacking because she listened to every word they said.

But as they started to drive away, the passenger rolled down his window and fired one shot, hitting her in the stomach. She died before she made it to the hospital.

Her father never found them. A cold case still to this day.

More tears poured out as she cried for both of her parents. For the loss of her childhood. Nothing was the same after her mom died.

Then Elliot came into her life. For a brief time, life had been happy again. Carefree. As if someone, other than her father, cared about her.

Maybe she clung to him a little too hard. Perhaps in an unhealthy way.

Like now.

She tried to shove out of his arms.

His grip tightened. "No, Emma. I'm here for you."

"It's not right. None of it is."

"It's okay. Everything is okay."

She grabbed the back of his shirt, squeezing hard. She wanted to shove out of his arms again. She wanted to run fast and hard. Something she had been doing the past six months since her father died. That's all she had been doing lately. Running.

Where had it gotten her?

Well, it finally brought her to a place she could maybe call home.

It brought her to Bentley.

"He lied to me."

Elliot tensed slightly. "Who?"

She wanted to let go, maybe even look him in the eye,

but she couldn't move. "My dad. He died of a heart attack. I was there. I saw it happen. I called the ambulance, but there wasn't anything anyone could do."

His hand rubbed her back a little harder. "I'm sorry you had to witness that. It's not easy. I was there when my mother passed away."

A tiny amount of strength finally found its way in, overshadowing her nerves. She leaned away to meet his gaze. "How did she die?"

"Cancer. She was in pain for a long time. It was difficult to watch."

"I'm glad he went quickly." She rolled her eyes. "I imagine he probably was, too."

"What did he lie about?"

"He was diagnosed with prostate cancer. He didn't have much longer to live. The heart attack took him before the cancer could. I found his medical bills that he was obviously trying to keep from me. He never said a word. My dad was dying and he never said one word."

"He loved you. He was probably trying to protect you. I can understand. Watching my mom go through all that pain was heartbreaking. I almost didn't survive."

She tried to wipe the tearstains from her face, a few drops still running down. "I want to hate him for it. I want to be so mad at him for leaving me all alone."

Elliot pulled her into his embrace again. "You're not alone. You'll always have me and Lynn...Bentley."

"I came here lost. I have no job. I have no place to live. I barely have any money. I'm a wreck. Bentley deserves better than a misfit like me."

Elliot chuckled. The light sound lifted the pain in her heart somewhat. "You have a job now. Lynn adores you and all the help you've been providing. When the baby comes, she'll need a lot more help in the bakery. You have a place to live. You are welcome to stay as long as you need. I have this feeling even Bentley would let you stay with him as long as you needed. If you need money, all you need to do is ask. I'm here to support you in any way I can." He sighed. "We're all a wreck at some point. You're not alone in that feeling. You deserve the best. As does Bentley. I honestly think you're perfect for each other. I haven't seen him this happy in a long time."

"You got this dad thing down." A low laugh escaped. His words started to fill the empty places in her soul.

"That's good to know because I swear every time Laura comes to me about something, especially boy related, I get so damn nervous I stutter."

Emma leaned away, a tiny grin appearing. "You're a wonderful father, Elliot. You're a wonderful friend. I think I feel a little better."

"Good. Then I feel better. Because I was worried about you. I still am. Don't hesitate to come to me about anything. I'm here for you. No matter what. No questions asked, if all you want to do is talk. I can listen."

She blew out a tiny breath and took a step back. He let her go. "I appreciate that."

Wiping more tears from her face, she glanced at the bed where her suitcase lay propped open, some clothes inside, and some waiting to be packed.

"It's okay if you go with him. Have some fun, Emma. Live your life. I have this feeling you've been holding back."

Boy, he had that right.

She never committed to anything, strolling through life with a fear so ingrained in her mind she didn't know how to let go.

"I look terrible. I can't walk out there now."

"If he truly cares about you, he's not going to care what you look like. Instead, he's going to ask why you were crying and try to make you feel better."

"You're really okay if I stay with him?"

Elliot nodded. "Him and I have an understanding."

She smiled. "Yeah, you had a little talk with him. He hurts me, you hurt him."

He winked as a soft chuckle floated between them. "And I will for any man you decide to date. Consider me your honorary uncle."

"I'm glad I decided to come here. Thank you, Elliot."

"I'm glad, too. You will always be welcome here."

Her smile stayed on her face even after Elliot walked out of the room. She glanced at all her belongings coating the bed, then continued to pack.

Supper went well. No interrogation ensued, although it wasn't necessary since Elliot already had the talk with Bentley. Gregory piped in with a few small warnings to Bentley, who laughed it off with his easygoing manner. But she knew Gregory was serious, as did Bentley.

They were stern in a friendly I-love-you-but-will-not-tolerate-nonsense kind of way.

She felt blessed to have found such wonderful people in her life. She almost wished she would've connected with Elliot a lot sooner than she did. Even before her dad died. Her dad would've loved to chat with Elliot about chief of police matters.

Before they all ventured into the living room for a cup of hot chocolate, Bentley whispered to her about spending the night.

That's why she fled to her room to pack.

But no more fleeing. No more running away from her problems.

She needed to start meeting them head on and dealing with them. Running never solved anything.

Wiping her cheeks a few more times to erase the evidence, knowing it probably didn't dent the atrocious look coating her face, she zipped up her suitcase.

She was going home with Bentley.

She was going to start letting him in.

She was done hiding behind her feelings.

And it all scared her shitless.

13

He honestly had no idea what he was doing. Playing it by ear, day by day, minute by minute, seemed like the best plan. Because creating a plan proved difficult. Every time he sat down on his bunk at the fire station to concoct the perfect surprise for Emma, he ended up scribbling it out. Nothing seemed good enough. She deserved the best surprise ever.

She deserved some happiness.

When she came out of her room last night with her suitcase in tow, he saw the tearstains that marred her cheeks. He didn't want to cause a scene in front of Elliot or Lynn, so he said nothing.

As soon as they got into his truck, she beat him to the punch, saying she had a small chat with Elliot about her dad, but she was okay. He didn't press the issue, even though he had wanted to.

He wanted to hear about her father. He wanted her to feel comfortable enough to talk to him about anything. Whatever they talked about had hurt her. Deeply. Her eyes had still been bloodshot from crying this morning.

He tried his best to cheer her up by making her breakfast. Nothing too fancy, since he wasn't some kind of gourmet cook, but eggs, toast, and bacon. A nice hearty meal to get her through until lunch.

That's when he came up with the brilliant plan to surprise her with something special. Something amazing. Something to put a beautiful smile on her face.

And he couldn't come up with a damn thing that sounded even close to wonderful.

Who was he kidding? He still hadn't thought of a good Christmas present for her. Talk about lame.

So, yeah. His plan was to play it by ear and hope a stupendous idea popped in his head in the moment.

He blew out a breath and opened the door to the bakery.

Lynn was behind the counter refilling the cookie display case. He smiled tentatively as he approached her.

"Good afternoon, Bentley. Need some goodies for the station?"

That wasn't a bad idea. Maybe that would soften the fire chief a bit. Every time they spoke, the fire chief was stern and to the point, unlike his usual laid back attitude. He knew he messed up by not following orders, but he still would've done the same thing no matter which way he looked at it. He saved that puppy's life. He made the little girl happy. He couldn't find fault in that.

"I'll take two dozen cookies. Thanks, Lynn."

She smiled, yet there was a sparkle of mischief in her eyes. "Is that your only reason for stopping by?" She started to bag his goodies as he debated how to answer.

"Umm...yes...and no. Did Emma have a lunch break yet?"

"She did."

A prime example of why it was a terrible idea to play it by ear.

"But it's been a slow day if you'd like to take her for a slice of pie or something."

He could use a slice of pie. Lunch wasn't the best of ideas, now that he thought about it. He had about twenty minutes until they headed out to deliver the presents from the Christmas party to the surrounding hospitals and shelters. The joy that spread across the kids' faces always filled his heart with happiness. He liked that he was a part of that special cheer. For a small time, those kids forgot about their illnesses, their pain, and focused on something special and exciting. A little Christmas spirit.

Then a light bulb went off.

"You know, I'd love pie, but I have another idea in mind. Do you think Emma would enjoy coming with to drop off the presents to the kids?" His eyes rounded, as his cheeks turned a hint of red. "That is, if you don't mind that she comes with. If she even wants to. Maybe she doesn't."

Lynn laughed softly as she set two boxes of cookies on the counter in front of him. "I think she'd love that. I don't mind. Like I said, it's been slow today."

A tiny breath escaped as he attempted to calm his racing nerves, and he couldn't even figure out why he was suddenly so nervous. Emma brought his emotions out like crazy, swirling and twirling, as if he were riding a merry-go-round and it wouldn't stop spinning.

He secretly loved it and hated it.

"Thanks, Lynn. I appreciate it."

He paid for the cookies, then ventured to the back of the bakery. A slow, lazy grin emerged as he watched her bag bread. It looked like a boring, mundane task, yet she made it appear sexy. Perhaps it was how her hair, tied up in a messy bun, was shoved in a hairnet, and her tongue sticking out the side of her mouth as if she were in serious concentration. It shouldn't have made her look an ounce of sexy, but to him, she was both the most adorable and the sexiest woman he had ever seen.

"That bread looks delicious."

Emma jumped, a hand touching her chest over her heart. Then sweet laughter floated out. "You startled me. How long have you been standing there?"

"Long enough to know you look so damn sexy bagging bread."

More sweet laughter filtered out. "Stop it. I look terrible."

"Never." He smiled wide as he moved closer to her. "So, I was wondering if you'd like to do something with me?"

"I'm pretty sure we already decided we were having pizza tonight. Did you change your mind?"

"I wasn't talking about that. I'm still making you my famous pizza."

A gentle smile touched her lips. It made him crave to trace his lips over hers. To taste her. To savor her. To see if she'd tried the delicious cinnamon swirl bread that she was bagging.

"Then what are you talking about?"

"Some of the guys and I are going to deliver Christmas presents to the local hospitals. For the children. I was wondering if you wanted to come with."

Surprise coated her eyes, yet her smile brightened. "I'd love to." Then she sighed. "I'm not sure I should leave Lynn."

His cheeks flamed, worry filling his veins. Would she be mad that he already spoke to Lynn about it?

Her brow rose. "You spoke to her already."

"How do you know me so well?" He smiled, hoping to ease the stern gaze on her face.

"I have no idea." She suddenly laughed. "But I do, so don't ever forget it, buster."

"Trust me, sweetheart. I never will." He laughed with her. "Lynn said it was okay."

Emma tied the last bag of bread, and then untied her apron. "Well, then, I would love to come with you. It's such a wonderful thing you do."

"The kids love it. I love seeing the excitement on their faces."

She met him on his side of the counter. "Where's my kiss?"

Wow. How did he live without this lively, vivacious woman for so long? He grabbed her around the waist and claimed her lips with his. He showed her exactly how much he'd missed her since this morning.

THE KISS SCORCHED her to the bone. Her body felt on fire, the desire burning through her veins like a raging inferno. She felt so alive. So hot for the man desperately holding her in his arms.

So hot.

Like a fire.

A blazing beast that could take his life at any time.

Her hands clutched the back of his jacket in a deadly grip. So tightly that if he tried to step away he wouldn't be able to escape.

She couldn't lose him, especially to a fire.

For the first time, his job and the danger it came with seared into her brain, refusing to leave. Her hands dug in further, her nails almost pinching his skin, her fear attacked her that strongly.

Yet, the kiss didn't slow down. If anything, it intensified, like flames consuming a building until it crumbled to the ground.

Now she understood why his boss was so furious with his actions. They were dumb and reckless. He could've died. She never thought about it until this very moment how dangerous his actions had truly been.

Biting his bottom lip, more aggressively than she'd intended by his soft moan of pain, she shoved him away slightly, yet her hands were still clutched to the back of his jacket.

"Don't you ever run into a burning building like that again. Do you hear me? Don't ever do anything so stupid again. I won't stand for it."

Bentley jerked in surprise as his tongue dragged across his bottom lip. "What brought that on?"

Her hands squeezed, her nails digging into his back again. He winced, but didn't try to push her away. "I won't lose you like that. Promise me." Her eyes narrowed. "You promise me right now you will not run into a burning building so recklessly ever again."

She couldn't explain her sudden terror at the thought of him risking his life for an animal. For anyone, for that matter. Maybe that made her a selfish bitch, but she didn't care. She couldn't lose him.

The fear refused to dissipate, especially when he said nothing in response. They held their gaze, her eyes dripping with fear, his coated with concern.

"It's my job, Em—"

"No!" Her nails pinched him harder. "You don't get to say things like that. You promise me right now. It's not your job to do dumb things. It was so dumb what you did."

His eyes lowered between them. She didn't miss the hurt that flashed in his eyes. "I didn't think it was dumb. I saved that puppy, and I'd do it again. I can't make that promise to you."

A cry tore from her lips as she pressed her head against his chest, inhaling his masculine scent that held a hint of smoke. Maybe that was a permanent part of him. Or maybe her mind conjured the smell because she still couldn't dislodge the fear etched permanently on her heart.

His arms wrapped around her tightly, his hot breath soothed her as it slid down her spine. A soft kiss on her neck followed.

"I'm sorry, Emma. Don't hate me. Don't push me away."

Her hands tightened once again. He was obviously getting used to her nails digging into his back because he didn't even flinch this time. "I want to hate you."

His breath hitched. "But you don't. Say you don't."

She buried her head even more in his chest, almost in the crook of his arm. "I never will."

Bentley let out a slow breath as he embraced her harder. "If you don't want to go today, I'll understand."

Inhaling a bout of strength, attempting to shove her fear to the back recesses of her mind, she backed away, her hands still locked tightly to his jacket. "I want to go." She inhaled deeply, then exhaled slowly as she let go of him. "I don't know what came over me. Forget what just happened."

She tried to shake off the craziness that tried to inhabit her body as she started to walk away. A hand snaked around her waist and pulled her back into his warm embrace.

"I know I don't have an easy job. It's not always safe. But I won't forget what happened. I can promise I'll always do my best. I know—" He stopped talking as he brushed a hand across her cheek. "I know it wasn't easy losing your dad. I don't want to say nothing will ever happen to me, because we never know what life has in store for us. But we have to talk about this stuff. You can't keep things bottled inside."

But it was easier to keep it inside. She learned so well how to do it. She didn't know how to talk it out.

But for Bentley, she would try. She nodded.

A grin touched his sexy lips. A tender kiss followed.

"We should go. Don't worry. You're going to love this."

He let go of her waist and grabbed her hand. She had no doubt she would. She trusted Bentley in that sense. But she didn't trust he would always be safe.

"I better. Or you'll see my wrath."

He chuckled as he started to lead her out of the bakery. "I love your wrath." He winked.

Laughter spilled from her lips. She didn't doubt he made her mad on purpose sometimes.

She couldn't be mad at him for how he felt about his job, even though she wanted to. He honestly couldn't promise her something he had no intention of keeping. She did respect him for that. She'd always rather have honesty than a bald-faced lie.

After throwing her hairnet away, she grabbed her coat, said goodbye to Lynn, and followed Bentley to the fire station.

As she watched him and his co-workers fill the big red fire truck with presents, her heart did a giddy little dance. Excitement tingled in her fingertips.

Bentley was right. She was going to love this.

Because seeing the happiness on those kids' faces, who didn't have a lot to smile about, just might help the darkness inside her ebb away. Life wasn't so bad for her. She had to remember that. Life could definitely be worse.

THE SILLY GRIN on his face had been etched onto his features since they arrived at the hospital. The moment he saw some kids jumping up and down in the waiting room right in front of the glass doors, the grin appeared and refused to disappear. Then he saw Emma start to hand out presents, and the grin grew wider.

Her happiness, the joy spread across her face as she talked with the kids, helped them open their presents, squealed in delight when they got something amazing, he knew right then. He felt it deep in his gut.

She was the one.

They'd had some rough patches so far, probably would have a few more to come, but he wasn't going to give up on her.

That's not what you did when you loved someone. You fought, battled, and fortified on until that person understood you wouldn't be leaving until everything was back to picture perfect.

He'd do exactly that. She would understand, because he would make her understand.

His heart skipped a beat as the memory from the bakery penetrated his mind. A shiver rushed down his spine as her fear touched him once again.

She had been so scared for him. Almost like she would've been happy to know he wouldn't be a firefighter. Not happening, of course. He loved his job. He wasn't quitting for anything.

He had gotten a ton of flack from almost everyone for

running back into the burning building. His parents had called the next day to give him hell for acting the way he did, then to promptly say they loved him. They didn't call often to reprimand him about his actions on the job.

His boss, of course, reamed him out.

Some people in town, just in passing, couldn't resist saying something about how irresponsible he'd acted.

Even Gregory, when he was at Elliot and Lynn's house for supper, had pulled him aside and gave him an earful about following orders and acting responsibly. Being the former fire chief, now retired, he listened to Gregory. He listened to everyone.

But he still would've acted the same way given the same circumstances.

He wasn't going to lie about it. Especially to Emma.

If they were going to start a relationship, he had to be honest with her. Always.

The worry that instantly flooded his veins when she voiced her displeasure and fear still struck him like a blow to the back of his head.

Would his job come between them?

Would she be able to date—maybe marry—a firefighter?

Marry?

He barely knew her for two weeks and the word marriage was popping in his head.

Oddly enough, that word wasn't giving him the jitters.

The thought of losing her was making him tremor with unease.

A hard hand slapped him on the shoulder, almost jarring some of the worry away, considering he was now focusing on the slight pain jogging through his shoulder. It didn't help he stood outside, the temperatures super low today, as he monitored the distribution of the gifts.

He could see Emma perfectly through the glass doors, her excitement still strong.

"You look pissed. What's wrong?"

Bentley glanced at Charlie, who had whacked him hard on the shoulder. Smoothing out the frown he hadn't realized he had formed, his silly grin reappeared, and he slapped Charlie hard on the back. "Nothing's wrong."

Charlie chuckled as he rotated his shoulder, getting the drift he whacked him a little harder than was necessary. "Emma seems to be enjoying herself."

"Yeah, it's nice to see everyone having so much fun. This is one of my favorite times of the year. The smile on those kids' faces..." His grin spread as he watched a little boy frantically rip open the long box to find a fire truck with all the bells and whistles on it. The nurses would probably get a headache from all the sirens and the sounds it played.

"So...you and Emma?"

Cocking a brow, he laughed. "Subtle much, Charlie?"

He shrugged. "Curious minds, dude. Just last week you had the hots for Daphne."

"Geez, did everyone know?"

Laughter bounced between them. "Dude, you weren't exactly shy about it. You were so obvious."

"And I'm not about Emma?"

Charlie's brows pleated together. "Yes and no. You clearly have the hots for her, but how badly?"

"What's it to you?"

"Touchy, touchy. I thought we were having a friendly chat."

Maybe his words came out a little more forceful than he'd intended, but he didn't want to dissect his feelings for Emma with someone else. If he wanted to, it would be with

Aiden, not Charlie, who happened to be his good friend and co-worker. He simply wasn't his best friend.

He clapped Charlie on the back again, this time softer. "Well, she's taken. By me. How's that for a chat?" He chuckled when Charlie laughed. "Let's close up the truck and get ready for the next hospital."

"You got it." Charlie nodded and walked away.

That was a development he didn't see coming.

He staked his claim. He made it known Emma wasn't available. Because that's exactly what he figured Charlie was angling for.

His eyes darted to her beautiful face and smiled as her head dipped backwards as if she were laughing deeply.

The other guys were seeing the beauty, the magnetic pull she had.

But it was too late.

She was all his.

Nobody's but his.

14

Flopping down onto the couch, she grabbed her ankles and started to rub, slowly rubbing until she hit her thighs.

What was she doing?

She should be having Bentley give her a nice rub down.

A light chuckle floated through the air as she heard soft sounds coming from the kitchen.

Well, as soon as he made supper, then she'd have him give her the ultimate massage.

Working hard all morning in the bakery, then all afternoon delivering toys, took a toll on her. She couldn't remember the last time she had worked so hard. Her body was as sore as if she'd lifted weights the entire day without a break. She honestly didn't do much heavy lifting, so she wasn't exactly sure why she felt so sore.

A hot bath would be great.

Resting her head back against the couch, her eyes drifted shut.

Wow. It felt...wonderful to be so tired. Like she was

contributing to something, to society for a change, instead of floating around from one dead end job to another.

Her lips curled into a smile as she snuggled into the couch.

A light tap to her shoulder jolted her. Sitting up straight, her heart pounded. When she connected her gaze with Bentley, who was laughing for some reason, she couldn't hold back her laughter.

"What's so funny?"

"You look like an angel sleeping." His grin deepened. "But you wake up like the devil. On alert and ready to attack."

Pressing her lips together to hold back more laughter, she gave him an evil eye. She shouldn't secretly love the things he said, even when that last statement didn't sound so sweet. Being compared to the devil sounded like an insult. But when he said it with a grin on his face, the laughter in his eyes, and the desire in his hands as his fingers softly rubbed her shoulder, she saw it as one of the most beautiful comments she had ever received.

"You think you're so charming."

"You know I am." He winked, then pulled her gently to stand. "Come on. The pizza will get cold. Then, how about a bath? A hot, relaxing bath?"

"How did you know I was thinking about that?"

"I read you well, sweetheart." His handsome smile intensified as he held out a chair for her to sit down, then scooted it in when she did. His hot breath slid down her spine with erotic intent when he leaned down and whispered in her ear. "Plus, you were mumbling in your sleep about how nice a bath sounded. Your wish is my command."

Biting her bottom lip, the smile she was trying to

suppress broke free anyway. Could this man possibly get any sweeter with his words?

Oh, she had so many wishes.

Could he grant them all?

Well, not all of them. She wished every day, of every minute, that her father was here.

And he never would be.

Suddenly the thought of spending Christmas without him hit her. It hit her so strongly she jerked in her seat. Shaking off the melancholy feeling before Bentley saw, she blew out a tiny breath and forced a smile on her face.

She had no idea why that popped in her head. Why sudden sadness had to touch her.

Bentley paused after placing a slice of pizza on her plate. "I know you think you're hiding your emotions from me right now, but you're not. Did I say something wrong? I didn't mean—"

"It's nothing you said." She shrugged as she picked up her slice of pizza. "Maybe it is."

"I take it back, then." His goofy grin, probably to lighten the mood, lifted some of the gloominess that tried to suffocate her.

"Please don't. I want my wishes you promised."

A corner of his lip lifted, giving him a crooked, sexy grin she almost couldn't resist. So much so, she wanted to shove the pizza aside and devour him instead.

He grabbed his own slice of pizza and took a bite before saying anything. "When you're ready, I'm here to listen."

She took a bite of pizza rather than answer that thoughtful comment. Delicious flavors swirled around as she chewed, savoring the homemade pizza he cooked for her.

She knew this. She knew Bentley would probably be the best listener there ever was.

But she wasn't ready to talk about her dad. She wasn't ready to bring painful things up when their relationship was so fresh and new.

Then she needed to stop bringing the negative thoughts to the surface where he would potentially question why her mood changed.

A lot easier said than done. She didn't know how to stop those thoughts. They popped up without warning. There wasn't a day that went by that her dad didn't penetrate her thoughts at least once.

They ate the pizza in a comfortable silence, surprisingly, after she almost killed the mood. Before she left, she would make sure he made his pizza for her again. He added pepperoni, extra cheese, onions, and olives, but she'd request mushrooms next time as well. She loved mushrooms. She even ate them out of the can, the entire can, on occasion.

Wait?

Before she left?

Was she still thinking about leaving?

She had nowhere to go. She put her dad's house on the market, and it sold fast. She donated and got rid of most of his stuff. The few things she couldn't part with and needed by her side, she had tucked in her trunk. The lease on her apartment ran out last month, and the lame job she had at the convenience store in her old hometown probably wouldn't hire her again.

She had no real job, no real place to live, and no connections to any place that she cared about.

So why was she still thinking she had to leave?

This town was perfect for her. She had friends. She had a job.

And she had Bentley.

He looked up from his plate and flashed one of his sexy, brilliant smiles. "What is that beautiful mind of yours thinking?"

She wiped her hands on the napkin on her lap. "That you owe me a bath."

Wiping his mouth with a napkin, he stood up and motioned for her to follow him. "This is going to be the best bath you've ever had."

Giggling, she followed him to the master bathroom that had a huge circular tub, perfect for a relaxing hot bath.

The water started gushing out. Bentley ran his hands underneath the flowing stream until he found the perfect temperature. Then he went to a closet in the corner of the room and pulled out a pink ball, tossing it into the water. It started to fizz and slowly dissolve.

"A bath bomb? Really?" She cocked a brow.

"Get naked." He slapped her ass and then removed his shirt. "And they're my sister's. She stayed with me for a few weeks this past summer when they were remodeling part of her house. She forgot a few things."

"I'll have to thank her."

Laughter coated the bathroom as they both got naked as fast as they could.

"Get in. I'll be right back."

She didn't argue, because she wanted the hot water to soothe her bones. It was an added bonus that Bentley decided to take a bath with her. She didn't expect him to do that. She thought she'd take a bath while he did...whatever he wanted.

Which, apparently, was to take a bath with her.

A sweet sigh left her mouth as she slid down in the bathtub. The water couldn't fill up fast enough. It was already doing wonders for her sore body.

Bentley came back into the bathroom, his glorious, naked body proudly on display, his erection jutting out, telling her how excited he was to take a bath as well.

Setting a condom on the edge of the tub, he then joined her in the water, positioning himself behind her. His arms circled her stomach and pulled her snug against him. He felt perfect and right and like everything she always dreamed about when she was a little girl thinking about her white knight.

Her eyes darted to the condom. "Thinking you're getting lucky tonight, are we?"

A kiss touched her neck. "A guy can hope, can't he?"

A soft murmur was her only response as his hands slid down her arms and to her front. His fingers tickled her most sensitive spot, playing, enticing, making her ache for more.

She didn't want to be teased. She didn't want to be worked up.

She wanted him.

All of him.

Moving forward, the water swishing all around, she twisted until she was facing him. "There will be no teasing in this bathtub."

His eyes glittered with desire. "Then what shall there be?"

The condom disappeared into her hand. The only sound in the bathroom was the rushing of the water as it continued to slowly fill the tub and the crinkling of the package.

"I need you." Her voice almost broke as she said it, the

meaning going a little deeper than she intended, as she slid the condom on him.

His arms wrapped around her waist as she maneuvered on his lap until he was deep inside her. He felt...made for her.

With her knees bent, water rising around them, straddled on him, she started moving. Not gently either. She rocked up and down, the water splashing to and fro.

"Damn, Emma, you feel so good."

A smile touched her lips before claiming his. The kiss turned hot immediately, almost as hot as the water, as his hands held her back tightly, her movements rough and fast.

She didn't care that the water splashed over the rim of the tub as she moved up and down. She didn't care about the mess they were creating. All she cared about was how wonderful his hands felt holding her tightly, how his kisses melted her senses, how glorious it felt to be connected as one with him.

Matching her movements, he started pumping his hips, digging deeper, making the intense desire building explode without warning.

Moaning loudly, as their lips refused to part, the bliss spread throughout her body. His hands tightened on her waist, moving her up and down a little faster, pumping as hard as he could.

The ecstasy flowed like electrical currents, like bolts of lightning zapping her body over and over as Bentley worked his way up to his own orgasm.

His fingers dug into her waist as it finally hit him. The kiss went wild as she enjoyed how his body tensed, his hands marking her, his touch branding her.

Slowly, the kiss softened, his hands soothing her as he rubbed her back.

"This is the best bath I've ever had."

Chuckling, she grabbed another kiss before sliding off him. "Well that sounds like a challenge. I'm sure we could do better."

He stood up, plucked the condom off, and tossed it in the garbage can sitting close to the tub. Sitting back down, he grabbed her around the waist and rested her against his chest.

His lips hit her neck. His soft touch soothed her almost better than the water. "Challenge accepted."

HE TOOK a swig of beer before turning to Aiden. "You know, last time we were here, these ladies were tearing the joint down with their drunkenness."

Aiden chuckled. "But look at them. They're having so much fun."

Bentley hadn't taken his eyes off Emma all night. That's all he'd been doing lately. Looking at her, reveling in her beauty, happy that he could call her his girlfriend.

He made sure all day at the fire station that everyone understood—not just Charlie—that she was off limits.

Charlie wasn't the only one yesterday who had looked at her with admiration and longing. Even a few men in the bar were giving her and Theresa looks, as if they had some sort of chance.

When Aiden asked if they wanted to grab a beer, he didn't hesitate. Well, much. He did want Emma to himself, but he knew that would be selfish. Plus, he needed more than just himself to show Emma she had a reason to stay.

His smile grew as he watched her laugh with Theresa. Something was obviously funny because they were laughing prettily heavily. He could only hope the more connections she made, the more friends she made, she'd be less inclined to leave.

The fear wouldn't dissipate, swallowing him whole every time he thought about her leaving.

He knew she didn't like to talk about, well, almost anything in her personal life, but they needed to soon.

Not only did he want to know everything about her, he wanted to help her with whatever was bothering her. And he knew a lot was bothering her.

Emma whooped loudly as she jumped in the air excitedly. He flashed a bright smile and winked when she looked at him with a sassy smirk and pointed to the dartboard where she had hit the bullseye.

Theresa had asked if Emma wanted to play, but now he wanted to play with her. He could tell she knew what she was doing. What a game it would be. He loved sparring with her. It didn't matter what it happened to be about.

But he wouldn't ruin their fun. This night out wasn't just about Emma. He knew Aiden wanted Theresa to get out more with other people. She was a big homebody, working on her jewelry most nights. On occasion, she liked to hang out with Lynn. He figured this was Aiden's way to get the ladies to become friends. Real friends.

It looked like his plan was working as they slapped hands after Theresa hit the spot she needed.

"Is that jackass out of town yet?"

"His bail hasn't been paid. He's still sitting in lockup with his busted leg." Aiden chuckled. "He keeps moaning and groaning about why he had to leave the hospital. His leg is wrapped up, so he didn't need to stay there anymore, but he doesn't get that. I wish he'd pay his bail. He's annoying everyone."

"I wish so, too."

Aiden took a drink, then eyed him curiously. "Did Emma say anything about him?"

"Not really. He cheated on her with her best friend. That's about it." He sighed. "She doesn't like to talk about...a lot of things. It's frustrating as hell."

"It seems serious between you two. She's not even staying with Chief Duncan anymore."

"You proposed to Theresa within less than a month of dating, so don't even go there." His voice might've been a little more stern than he intended, but he wasn't about to hear dating advice from his friend who didn't follow the same practice.

Aiden's hands went up in surrender. "I wasn't going to say anything. If it's right, it's right." His eyes swiveled to the ladies. "But, be careful. I don't want to see you get hurt."

He didn't respond. He had nothing witty, or even serious, to say.

Because he didn't want to get hurt either. The fear weaving its way through his veins, taking permanent residence, said it might happen.

"Daphne asked me to help set up the reception," Aiden said casually.

A sigh of relief almost escaped, but he held it in because he didn't need Aiden questioning him. He still hadn't said a word to Emma about it. How would she react? Would it even matter to her? It wasn't a big deal.

"Yeah, me, too."

Aiden cocked a brow. "Is Emma helping, too? Theresa's coming with me."

He shrugged, avoiding eye contact. "I haven't mentioned it yet."

A low chuckle floated between them. "I knew it. What

are you doing, man? One guy already cheated on her. She's probably a lot more cautious. You need to talk to her about it."

"What's the big deal?" Groaning, he rubbed a hand down his face. "I didn't even date Daphne. Well, not for long and it was in high school. It's not a big deal."

"But you had a huge crush on her. So huge the entire town knew about it. Who says that crush disappeared?" Aiden held up his hands in an innocent gesture. "I can see it has. But can Emma? Don't keep these little things from her. It might not seem like a big deal, but it is."

Damn it. He knew Aiden was right.

How would she react when he mentioned it? Would she demand he not help? Because he saw it as a possibility. While he didn't see Daphne as a woman he wanted anymore, she was still his friend. He didn't want to lose that.

As his eyes connected with Emma's, a sweet smile lighting her face, he knew what woman he wanted.

Her.

Only her.

He hoped she believed him.

15

She shoved on her hot pink knit mittens, wishing her hat matched her mittens instead of being a boring cream color, then grabbed the big box of cookies resting on the counter. Although a dull color, her knit hat already felt better than the stupid hairnet she had to wear while in the bakery. She understood the need for the thing, but it didn't mean she liked putting it on every day. Half the time it made her forehead itch, which was something she tried hard to avoid.

Thinking about it made her want to scratch her head right in that moment, but instead, she shoved the inkling away, said a quick goodbye to Lynn, and stepped outside the bakery.

Bonzo, the owner of the diner where Theresa worked, needed a refill of cookies. The town loved baked goodies from Lynn. Bonzo was not dumb. He had her supplying the bakery with cookies, sometimes pies, when she first opened.

The diner was only two doors down from the bakery, so she probably didn't need to bundle up as she did, but the temperatures were dipping lower every day. The heavy snowfall everyone was waiting for still hadn't arrived.

Plus, she loved her hat and mittens. It brightened her day when sometimes there was nothing bright to it.

Of course, she couldn't say today wasn't bright. Bentley made her pancakes and then showered with her before they both ventured off to work. What wasn't bright about that?

She loved the morning routine they had. She even loved the evening routine.

She loved it all.

Loved...him?

She jerked to a stop, a few steps away from the diner door. The last person she wanted to see stood in front of her.

"You're a long way from home. What do you want, Ashley?"

The woman who called herself her best friend for eleven years smiled, no malice within the depths.

But that was the problem. She didn't display that before she decided to sleep with her boyfriend. She simply did and kept on pretending as if she was her best friend.

"Jared called me. I'm here to pay his bail."

"Have fun doing that." She took a step forward, hoping to make Ashley take a step back, but she didn't budge.

"How come you didn't pay it?"

A chuckle left her mouth at the ridiculous question. "Why in the hell would I?"

"He came here for you. He wants you back."

Emma couldn't stop the wide smile that spread across her face at Ashley's poutiness. That's exactly how she heard it, too. Like a little child whining because their toy was taken away. Ashley could have Jared with open arms. Good riddance.

"How did you know I was here? How did he know?"

Ashley rolled her eyes, just like she used to do when they would go to the mall and people watch, laughing and making fun of others to themselves. On occasion, Ashley would get a little too loud for her tastes. That's usually when Emma told her it was time to go.

"Were you trying to be all cloak and dagger about it? In case you forgot, we did live together. We were both on the same lease and—"

"How could I forget, you moved out when you started sleeping with Jared, leaving all the payments to me."

Ashley rolled her eyes again. "And," she emphasized, "the landlord told me you left an address when you asked him if you could leave some of your belongings in his garage. That doesn't explain where all my stuff went."

A wily smirk emerged as she shrugged. "I figured you didn't want anything after you left. You didn't even call to apologize for stealing my boyfriend. I figured all that stuff was a consolation prize. You took all your clothes and personal items, everything else left in the apartment, we bought together. So I had every right to get rid of it the way I saw fit."

She sold the big stuff, like the table and chairs, and donated the rest. She couldn't afford to rent a big storage unit for her dad's belongings and the few personal things she wanted to keep, so she braved trusting another person. Her landlord, Steve, had always been a decent guy. He lived in the same building, but his parents didn't live too far away, so she asked if she could keep her things in their garage until she found a new place to stay. Even though the memories in that apartment haunted her at times, seeing her best friend the way she used to be, she would've continued to live there if she could've afforded it. But by herself, it hadn't been possible.

"What are you doing in this Podunk town?"

An incredulous laugh burst free. "Excuse me? Like the town we grew up in isn't Podunk. Shut your mouth. They're great people." Her eyes narrowed. "And what I do is none of your damn business."

"What about Jared?"

This time she rolled her eyes. "I'm not sure why you think I'd want that asshole back. He can rot in jail for all I care."

"He was the breadwinner for you. He wants you back. You're going to throw that away? I highly doubt it."

Ashley's words speared her like a knife to the gut. Was that how he saw her? Was that why he cheated on her with Ashley? She didn't argue when he wanted to pay for things, for some of her bills on occasion, but she never sought him out about it. She never *asked* him to pay for her things. Did that make her some kind of gold digger? She didn't think so.

She inhaled a sharp breath. The cold air burned her throat.

Did Bentley see her like that? Like she was using him.

In a way, she was.

She had a job, sure. But she didn't pay him rent. She didn't buy any groceries, although, she had yet to see him go to the store.

Well, she'd buy them when he decided it was time. Or, better yet, she'd grab some groceries on her way home.

She wasn't a gold digger. She wasn't someone who pawned off someone else.

She was on her own. She would make it on her own.

No matter what Ashley said, she did not rely on a boyfriend to get her through life.

"Just as I thought." Ashley took a step forward. Her eyes finally flashed with the devious evil she knew was hidden inside her. "He's mine. You can't have him."

"He's all yours. Get the hell out of my face and don't bother me again."

A smile appeared out of thin air, as if she never laid down her version of the law. "You're nothing without us, Emma. You're a loser, and you always will be." Ashley spun around and walked away.

A loser.

She felt like one for becoming friends with such a bitch. For dating a man that would turn his back with one little sultry smile from another woman.

She should've known. Her dad always got a certain look when she talked about Ashley. He had a gut feeling even when they first became friends that she would be trouble. Like the rebellious teenager she could be, she ignored every word out of her dad's mouth. She latched onto Ashley as her best friend and didn't look back.

Well, she'd start looking back now. She'd learn from her mistakes.

She owed it to her dad.

"Sorry, Dad. You were right," she whispered under her breath.

A strong gust of wind blew into her back as she pulled open the door to the diner. A melancholy feeling swept through her. But so did a strange sense of peace, as if that gust of wind was her father giving her forgiveness.

"Are you okay?"

Theresa's concerned expression made some of the anguish drift away as she took a seat at the counter and set the box of cookies down.

"Yeah, I think I am."

"Who was that woman?" Her cheeks turned a light shade of red. "If you don't mind me asking. It's really none of my business."

"Are we friends, Theresa? Like, real friends?"

Theresa's concern melted away as her eyes lit up with eagerness. "I think so. I hope so."

Emma's smile matched Theresa's. Big, wide, and so infectious they both started to giggle. "Well, then, let me tell you all the juicy details about that bitch."

HE SHUT THE DOOR QUIETLY, then locked it. Hanging up his jacket, his stomach gurgled loudly as the delicious smells hit his nose. Following the wonderful scent, he found Emma in the kitchen in front of the sink washing dishes.

The smell intensified, making his stomach gurgle even more.

"What's cooking? And what is the occasion?" Bentley laughed as he snagged an arm around Emma's waist and pulled her in for a kiss.

How did he get so lucky to meet such a beautiful woman?

Her wet hands landed on his chest as a sweet smile punctured her gorgeous face. "I picked up some groceries and decided to make lasagna. It's my mom's famous recipe. It probably won't taste like hers." Her eyes shifted down as her smile dipped some. "Not that I remember what it tastes like, but my dad said it was heaven. The best meal she ever made."

"It smells delicious. My mouth is literally watering right now."

Her gaze met his. “Well, I hope you like it.”

Strange.

She was acting…insecure. The Emma he had come to know never displayed an ounce of insecurity.

Something must’ve happened, and he had a strong inkling what.

“Sorry I’m late. It happens sometimes. We had to help a family of four trapped in their car after they slammed into the ditch hard. I hope you weren’t waiting on me too long.”

She grabbed a kiss before twisting out of his arms to finish the dishes. “Nope. The lasagna has another twenty minutes, at least. Is everyone okay?”

He nodded. “They’re shaken up. I think the mom broke her leg and the little boy has a gash on his head. Their car is totaled, but I guess that doesn’t matter at the end of the day as long as they’re alive.”

“You’re a hero again.”

A chuckle sprinkled around the kitchen. “I don’t see it like that. I’m doing my job.”

She paused, her hands submerged in the water, her eyes twinkling with awe, a delicate smile on her face. “But you are. You help people. You try to keep them safe. That’s a hero to me. That’s what my dad did every day. He’s a hero, too.”

That was the second time she talked about her family. Something she rarely did.

He wasn’t sure exactly what was going on, but he didn’t want her to stop sharing. He wanted her to let him in, and apparently, she decided it was time.

But he had no idea what to say. The wrong move could change the course of the evening.

“I love my job. I don’t see it as being a hero. I bet your

dad loved his job, too. He sounds like he was a great guy." He sucked in a breath and held it, waiting for her response.

"Oh, he loved his job." Her eyes drifted to the sink as she continued to wash a bowl. "A little too much sometimes." Their eyes connected. "Is that how it's going to be with you?"

He felt like so many different emotions and conversations were floating between them, as if she couldn't decide what one to stick with.

Her insecurity.

Her admiration.

Her fear.

He had no idea which one to tackle first.

"I can't see myself doing anything else. I'll be a firefighter until I retire. And yeah, I work shitty hours and I'll be home late sometimes." He took a step closer to her and pulled her into his arms once again. She barely resisted, yet he could feel the tension coiling her body. "But you're important, too. I can balance both things."

"I think my dad thought the same thing." Her mouth dipped into a frown. "But he sucked at it."

His grip around her waist tightened, as though he thought if he didn't hold her tightly, he'd lose her. She'd slip away and never come back again.

"What's going on here? Did I do something wrong?" He inhaled a deep breath. "Is this about...your visitor today?"

Boy, he hoped he didn't screw up by mentioning her ex-friend Ashley. With the way her eyes narrowed into tiny slits, looking at him like she was ready to gut him from head to toe, it might've been the wrong move.

"How do you know about that?"

A tiny chuckle escaped before he could stop himself. "It's a small town. She bailed out Jared, and from there, the news cycled around. Daphne said—"

He stopped speaking when her eyes turned to icicles.

"Daphne said what? Please elaborate."

"She said Ashley had a few choice words about you... and...she might've seen you two talking outside the diner. What did she say to you?"

"So, what, big mouth Daphne had to tell everyone?"

"She didn't mean it in a malicious way. She likes to talk and—"

Emma shoved out of his arms and moved to the opposite side of the kitchen. "I don't like to be the subject of gossip. The fact I didn't know people were talking means they didn't want me to know. Like I'm some laughingstock of the town."

"No one was laughing at you." His lips thinned into a straight line. "If anything, they were protecting you. They made sure—from Daphne to the officer that released Jared to the gas station attendant when they filled up her car—that they left town quickly. The town banded together to protect you."

"I knew there was a reason I didn't like small towns. I told myself I would move to a big city after I saw Elliot."

His heart started to pound. His hands started to twitch. His nerves started to jangle like a bunch of tiny elves ringing bells.

"Is that what you plan to do after Christmas? Move to a big city?"

Her shoulders slumped. "I don't know what I want to do." She surprised him when she moved closer and wrapped her arms around him, resting her head on his chest. "I just know my world feels better when I'm with you."

His arms tightened around her, but the nervous anxiety rushing through his veins wouldn't dissipate.

He still hadn't mentioned helping Daphne with her reception. Now didn't seem like the ideal time.

But he would.

He'd do it before it was too late.

16

Emma pulled the pan of pies out of the oven and set it carefully on the counter. Resisting the urge to rub her forehead and whip off the annoying hairnet, she shoved another pan of pies into the oven.

Lynn wanted to stock up as much as possible today. Because she loved the holidays so much, she planned to open in the morning tomorrow for Christmas Eve. People needed goodies.

She couldn't believe how fast time went.

Her time was almost up.

Well, if she decided to leave. She still hadn't made up her mind.

Every night, lying in Bentley's arms, she made the choice to stay, to build a life with him.

Every morning, after leaving to go their separate ways, the doubt crept in.

Was she relying on another person again? Did she need to venture out on her own first to see if she could survive? Did she want to be a part of another small town that didn't know how to mind their own business?

She didn't know what she wanted.

She couldn't wait to go home, take a shower, or even a relaxing bath, and snuggle in front of the TV with Bentley. A nice, quiet evening before all the hoopla started. Oh, she enjoyed Christmas and all the festivities it came with, but this year would be different.

She'd be surrounded by tons of people. Elliot invited her and Bentley over for Christmas Eve in the evening and for lunch on Christmas day. In the evening on Christmas day, they planned to go to Bentley's parents' house.

That made her nervous. She had never met a guy's parents before. What did she wear? What would she say?

She felt so lost. Like she was drifting in the middle of the ocean on a piece of wood with no land in sight. Drifting for days, the hot sun beating down on her. The water enticing her to drink, to hydrate herself. Yet, she resisted, knowing the outcome would lead her to nothing but madness.

And, of course, the other thing she didn't want to think about.

Daphne was getting married tomorrow morning. Elliot invited her to join him and his family—with Bentley.

She almost said no. But she knew how it would look, and she didn't want to give the town more to talk about.

What did she have against Daphne?

Bentley was all hers.

He was.

If she repeated it enough in her head, she might actually start to believe it. Because she hated to admit how much the insecurity entered when she thought she was nothing more than a distraction for him because Daphne was getting married.

She couldn't be. He would never treat her so callously.

What did he see in Daphne, anyway? Who got married

on Christmas Eve? She still thought that was the dumbest thing ever.

The ceremony would be in the morning, followed by a reception with a lunch fit for any Christmas Eve affair. The party would end in time for everyone to do their own thing in the evening. Daphne didn't want to take away from the Christmas festivities the entire day...ha! Just half the day.

Talk about selfish.

Her hand paused swiping more frosting on a cookie.

Or was she being selfish?

The last two weeks, besides the moments she let her insecurity surface, had been perfect. Bentley had been the supreme gentleman, doting on her like she was his everything.

Maybe she was.

Maybe she was letting this Daphne business make her decision for her.

Slapping the frosting on the cookie, she tried to let all the doubts filter away.

"How are the pies coming along?"

Emma jerked her attention to the doorway, surprised she didn't hear Lynn step inside her domain. Because, for the past week, she normally worked hidden in the back, away from prying eyes. She only ventured to the front when Lynn really needed her help. Perhaps Lynn knew she wasn't much of a people person. She preferred not to work the front counter. Not to mention, there was a lot of heavy lifting she did back here, the work more strenuous, something she didn't want Lynn to be doing seven months pregnant.

"I loaded another batch into the oven. They're all looking and smelling delicious."

Lynn smiled. "Great. We should hopefully be done on time. I'm sure you don't want to be late for tonight."

Emma's brows puckered as the confusion settled in. "Late? Did I miss something on the itinerary? Because this holiday is the most jammed packed I've had in a long time." She lightly laughed, almost happy it was so busy.

Yet, she still felt overwhelmed by it all.

Lynn's mouth formed a wide circle, but her eyes stayed connected with hers as the worry started to form. "I thought Bentley asked you to help. I know Aiden and Theresa are. Elliot and Gregory are showing up, too. They're setting up Daphne's reception tonight."

All about Daphne again.

And Bentley didn't tell her. Now she looked like a fool.

A laugh left her mouth, although she knew it sounded fake. "See, I told you I couldn't keep up with everything planned. I forgot about that."

Lynn smiled, yet she knew Lynn wasn't fooled. Bentley didn't tell her, and she knew it. "Those pies smell great, but I'm ready to go home soon."

"Yeah, me, too."

She was almost ready to leave altogether.

Bentley lied to her.

He watched in silence as Emma packed her bag. Not neat and organized either, but haphazardly throwing her belongings in the suitcase, not caring they would get wrinkled.

He messed up. Big time.

Every time he thought about telling her that he was helping Daphne with her reception, the time didn't feel right. Now, here it was. In less than an hour, he had to head to the hotel to help set up.

Time ran out.

He should've told her. It shouldn't have been a big deal, yet by not telling her, he made it into a big deal.

Maybe she would've said, "Yeah, okay. That's cool." Maybe she would've helped without an issue, especially knowing Theresa would be there. Those two had become good friends in a short time. Emma either took her daily lunch with Lynn in the back of the bakery or headed to the diner and spent her time with Theresa.

Now he'd never know how she would've reacted because he waited too long to tell her.

"I'm sorry, Emma. It slipped my mind. I meant to tell you."

Her movements stalled, but she didn't look at him. "There's a reason you didn't tell me."

"No. I..." Damn it, she was right. There was a reason. He didn't think she'd like it. "Okay, I was worried how you'd react."

Her eyes jerked to his. "Well, now you see how I'm reacting when you hide something from me."

"By running." His hand whipped to her suitcase.

"By taking some space. I'm staying with Elliot until..."

His heart skipped a beat. "Until you decide to come back here...or leave for good?"

"Why did you think I'd react badly?"

He looked away, afraid to answer. But he wasn't a coward. If he could run into a burning building for a puppy, he could look her in the eye. "Because, for some reason, you don't like Daphne. Just hearing her name, you cringe. I don't want to lose you over something ridiculous like me helping her set up her reception. She's my friend. It's nothing. I'm helping a friend."

"I cringe, because she's the other woman. I cringe, because you used to pine over her. Don't try to deny it because the entire town will corroborate it." Her brows bent low as her expression turned fierce. "It's not ridiculous. You don't understand why I'm even upset. It's not because you want to help, because I know the nice guy you are. It's because you lied to me. You hid it from me. I had to find out from Lynn and pretend I knew what the hell she was talking about. You made me look like a fool." She sighed, as if the fight inside her was dying. She zipped up the suitcase. "I've already been made a fool of once by my best friend. I won't let it keep happening."

"I won't deny I had a thing for Daphne, but that was nothing compared to what I feel for you. I swear it, Emma. You mean so much to me."

She set her suitcase on the floor. "You have a funny way of showing it. I need space, Bentley. I need time to think."

That was something he didn't want to give her. He didn't think her decision would be in his favor when she finished ruminating about it.

He screwed up, and he would do anything to make it up to her.

"I don't need to help tonight. Stay. We'll work this out. We'll talk. We'll do whatever you want to do."

Walking up to him slowly, she laid a hand on his chest. "And make me look like a colossal bitch by not showing up. No, thank you. Go and help. I'll be at Elliot's."

A shiver rippled through her body, attacking him in the same manner. It's as if her sadness zapped him straight to the core. He didn't just screw up. He ruined the best thing that had ever happened to him.

He knew it without a doubt as she let her hand fall from his chest and walked out of his bedroom without glancing behind once.

The front door closed.

Silence surrounded him.

Loneliness engulfed him.

He had the best woman in the world in his arms. Now he had nothing.

What a merry Christmas.

17

Shivering, she rubbed her hands over the steering wheel, thankful her car decided to start. When she twisted the key, the nerves almost overwhelmed her that it wouldn't start. She had gotten in the habit of riding with Bentley around town. She hadn't tried to start her car in over two weeks.

Relying on him. Over and over.

Well, she wouldn't be relying on him ever again. She couldn't even trust him to tell her the truth.

She honestly couldn't say how she would've reacted to hearing he would be helping Daphne. Probably not too harshly. She didn't want to look like a bitch to the town. That reaction sounded bitchy.

As she slowed down to turn into Elliot's driveway, she hesitated. Wasn't leaving Bentley's, fleeing to Elliot's, not helping, just as bitchy?

Time and again, Bentley pointed out how the town cared about her. Daphne, although sickeningly sweet every time they talked, had never been rude. She never displayed maliciousness behind the depths of her sweetness. She hated to admit she didn't think any of it was an act. Daphne was just a nice, sweet person. Quite annoying to her, but nice and sweet, nonetheless.

How could anyone be so nice all the time? Didn't she get exhausted?

Emma felt exhausted just thinking about it. Not that she considered herself a mean person, but she didn't go out of her way to put on a nice front every second of the day like Daphne.

Now what would the town think about her? How would they react?

Letting her foot off the brake, she eased it to the gas pedal and drove past Elliot's.

She couldn't stick around. Not anymore.

As soon as Bentley showed up without her, she'd be kicked out of the tight-knit town that had formed around her when she arrived. By not showing her support of Daphne, one of the town sweethearts, no one would forgive her.

It was better to leave now. Why wait?

She'd call Elliot once she arrived, wherever she decided to stop, and let him know she was okay. Let him know how sorry she was that she wouldn't be around for Christmas.

They wouldn't miss her that much. They all had each other. They had for a long time. Not many people noticed when she wasn't around. She didn't think they'd be any different.

It was time to stop letting life control her and control it instead. She would rely only on herself. No other man. No other woman. No other person at all.

If she needed to live in her car, that may or may not make it another five miles, she would. Thanks to Lynn, she had a bit of money saved up. Hopefully it would last her until she could find a new job.

Big city, here I come.

She could meld into the crowd and be another person living her own life.

Her phone buzzed on the passenger seat.

Her hands, wrapped in her hot pink mittens, tightened around the steering wheel.

Looking would serve no purpose. It didn't matter who was calling.

She'd made her decision.

She was leaving town.

BENTLEY SHOVED his phone into his pocket, then zipped his jacket and headed outside.

He only needed to give her space. After some time, not too much time, she'd be amicable enough to talking everything through. Hopefully, anyway. She had to forgive him. He didn't want to think about the alternatives if she didn't.

When he walked into the ballroom, he nearly turned around and walked out. He didn't want to explain why Emma wasn't by his side.

A smile wouldn't even produce as he joined Aiden and Theresa by Daphne and her fiancé.

"Where's Emma?" Daphne asked with the sweetest smile. There was rarely a time when he didn't see a smile on her face. Right now, that was the last thing he wanted to see. His stomach gurgled with unease as her smile didn't waver.

"She...isn't going to make it. Where should we start?" He clapped his hands, forcing a smile of his own out so no one would pelt him with questions.

Daphne's smile wavered for a fraction of a second, then she pointed to the round tables against the wall. "I need six chairs around each table. I have seating arrangements, so I'd like name cards set up when we're done arranging everything the way I want it."

He nodded, then listened intently as Daphne explained how she wanted the tables set up. He got to work right away, hoping the exertion would push away the melancholy mood that wanted to take over.

"So, where is she?" Aiden whispered as they grabbed a table together.

A sigh escaped as his fingers tightened on the table. "She left. Not officially, but she went to Elliot's. I might've failed to mention tonight. She's pissed at me for...lying."

"After what happened with her last boyfriend, I can see why she's upset."

Bentley slammed the table down hard, not even caring how loud it sounded, or that it attracted attention. His patience was run dry. "Thank you, oh wise one, for your input."

"Hey, you can be pissed at me all you want, but you know you should've told her."

"Yeah, Aiden, I know. You don't need to tell me. I screwed up." A hand ran down his face as he made his way to grab another table. "I'm not sure it would've mattered in the long run. I don't think she was ever really mine. She doesn't want to live in a small town again. She wants the big city life."

"So wish her luck and move on. You'll find the perfect woman when it's the right time. Maybe it's just not now."

"Where is the advice I want? Everything you're saying is complete bullshit. She is the perfect woman for me. Come on, man. Act like my best friend and come up with a solution like you did with Theresa. Not this other crap."

Aiden pursed his lips, as if contemplating his next words. Bentley didn't want that, he wanted it said straight.

"Spit it out."

"I don't want you to pine over Emma like you did over Daphne. You clung to her for a long time instead of looking for another woman to make you happy. I'm afraid you'll mourn over Emma far longer than you ever did with Daphne."

Mourn? That was an interesting choice of words.

But it made sense. That's how he felt right now.

Like he'd lost a piece of himself. She took a part of his heart when she walked out of the house. He would never be whole again unless she returned.

That was definitely something to mourn over.

"I love her. I don't think I'll ever love another woman like I do her. This can't be the end. I have to make it up to her somehow."

A tentative smile slowly grew on Aiden's face. "Well, we can think of something. But you can't take my mistletoe idea because Emma knows about it. You gotta be original."

"You're the romantic, apparently. Come up with something good."

Aiden laughed as they grabbed another table together. "You have to help. Emma's smart. She'll know whether it was your idea or not."

Setting another table down more gently than the last one, he chuckled. "She totally would. Okay, I'll think as we work. Something will come to me. I need to win her over before the night's over. I don't even want to know how empty my bed will feel tonight."

Aiden made a cringe worthy face, as if the very idea sounded preposterous.

Bentley clapped him on the back, hard, just to erase the

nasty look. Because it made his stomach churn with unease that he would be spending the night alone.

He paused in his steps when he saw Elliot walk into the ballroom with Gregory in tow. Was he here to talk about Emma? To help? He almost didn't want to know the answer, but he was about to find out as Elliot stopped in front of him.

The smile on his face gave him hope.

"Hey, Bentley." Elliot glanced around the room. "Where's Emma?"

At the innocent question, the hope slowly withered away and died.

Then he froze. Every muscle in his body.

His heart started to race like a lunatic smashing everything in their path.

"What do you mean? She's at your house."

She had to be. She said she was going to Elliot's.

Did she lie to him?

Did she leave already?

Elliot's smile disappeared as concern coated his eyes. "Emma's not at my house. Why would you think that?"

"She...we..." Bentley swallowed hard. "We had a small argument. She packed up her things and said she'd be staying with you until the holidays were over. She didn't go to your house? She left before I came here."

Elliot pulled his phone out and dialed a number. Bentley didn't even need to ask who he was calling.

Emma.

To find out why she never showed.

He thought he screwed up big time. He couldn't even find the right word for how badly he messed up.

She didn't just leave his house.

She fled town.

Elliot dropped the phone from his ear when he didn't receive an answer and then dialed another number. Bentley listened as he spoke to Lynn, telling her to call him if Emma showed up or called her.

"We'll find her."

The encouraging look on Elliot's face should've soothed his worries, but it did nothing but reinforce how badly he messed up.

"And then what? She wasn't happy here."

Elliot put an arm around his shoulder and walked away from Aiden. Bentley couldn't tell if this was a good or bad thing. He wasn't sure he was ready to be reamed out by Elliot for hurting Emma. He'd never be ready for that. He never meant to hurt her.

"She was happy. She is happy. She's...still trying to work through losing her dad. I think she's overwhelmed by a lot of things. You have to stay patient with her. We all do. We're her family now. I always stick by my family. Do you understand, Bentley?" Elliot squeezed his shoulder. "You have to ask yourself how much you care about her."

"I don't need to. I love her."

Elliot grinned. "I figured as much. We all screw up from time to time. It's how you fix your mistake that counts. Give her time."

"She asked for some space. I'm going to have a hard time giving that, especially knowing she left."

"I know. But maybe that's what she needs right now."

Bentley tensed when Daphne approached them.

"Hey, Chief Duncan. Thank you so much for coming." She lightly laughed. "You two look so serious. Is everything okay?"

He needed to stop pretending. He needed to start being honest, and it had to start with Daphne.

"Not really, Daph. Emma isn't here tonight because I never told her I was helping you because I didn't know how she'd react. Because..." He inhaled a breath and let it out slowly. "Because I had a crush on you for a long time and she knew it. But what I felt for you was never close to what I feel for her, and I didn't tell her that enough. Now she's upset at me because I lied."

Daphne laid a tender hand on his arm. "I know that, Bentley. But I think you know that we were never meant for each other. For some reason, you liked to use me as an excuse not to find the right woman. Can I help somehow?"

"When we find her, maybe. But we don't know where she is. She said she was going to Elliot's, but never showed up. She left."

Daphne's hand squeezed his arm gently, offering him some comfort he desperately needed. Elliot's arm still clung around his shoulder. The people that cared about him were holding him together when all he wanted to do was fall apart.

"She's tough. She'll be okay." Daphne frowned in concern. "I hope she calls someone when she gets where she's going. Her vehicle isn't the best."

Elliot dropped his arm. Bentley felt the loss immediately.

"What do you mean?" Elliot asked, a bit too harshly. Bentley didn't miss the hint of panic in his tone.

"Well, I don't think it always likes to start. Bernie mentioned how he saw her trying to start it and it wouldn't crank right away." Daphne turned to him. "I thought you knew since she always drove around with you."

He had no idea. She never told him.

Elliot's slight panic transferred to him with a full-blown roar. "I need to find her. I need to find her now. It's freezing outside. It's starting to snow. What happens if it dies? What if—"

Elliot's hand clamped onto his shoulder tightly, his fingernails almost digging in. "We all need to stay calm. I'll contact dispatch and see if they've seen her drive by and tell them to keep an eye out for her. But we need to stay calm."

Calm.

Yeah, he didn't know if that would be possible.

He was far from calm.

His racing heart, his trembling nerves wouldn't even begin to calm down until he knew Emma was safe.

18

Her hands gripped the steering wheel hard. The snow coming down like sparkling white lights was almost pretty.

Except she couldn't appreciate the beauty as her mind tumbled around in circles. Like a vicious cycle.

Leave.

Don't leave.

Leave.

Don't leave.

Her phone wouldn't stop ringing.

First Bentley. Then Elliot. Even Lynn a few times.

Not once did she answer. What would she say? That she was a coward. That she excelled at running from anything difficult in life.

Perhaps that's why her dad didn't tell her he was sick. Maybe he feared she'd run away to make his passing easier. Instead, he went quickly. Maybe his body knew she'd survive that better.

But did she?

She still ran.

Rather than face her emotions, she kept ignoring them. Pretending everything would get better if she just pressed on. Nothing would get better if she didn't start to own her feelings.

Her anger.

Her sadness.

Her regret.

The car skidded to the right. Gripping the steering wheel even harder, she settled her car back to normal, avoiding the ditch.

The snow might appear beautiful in the twinkling dark night, but it was starting to make the roads a bit dangerous, especially in her ratty old car that needed new tires, like, two years ago.

She couldn't afford to crash her car.

Ha! Who was she kidding? She could barely afford to live on her own.

She couldn't afford to lose everything either.

Leaving this town meant losing a part of herself she didn't know had been missing for a long time.

Happiness.

This time, instead of her car jerking to the right, it started to make funny noises. Sputtering, smoke rising, she watched in horror as her car slowly died and stopped. Right in the middle of the road.

Her heater worked on the best of days. Today wasn't one of them.

The cold air seeped into her bones immediately. Her hands turned to icicles, like touching metal on a cold wintry day.

She had worried about crashing her car. No need when she could freeze to death.

Well, she hoped she had some luck on her side. She

wished upon a star that another car would drive by soon and give her a ride back to town.

Guess she wasn't leaving so soon after all.

BENTLEY COULDN'T HELP IT. He constantly stopped what he was doing to look at Elliot to see if one of his officers had seen or heard anything about Emma.

Every time, he shook his head and went back to his task.

Daphne's infectious smile made him work harder to get everything set up, so he could do his own searching for Emma. Not that he knew where to look. But he couldn't let Daphne down. He promised to help and he would. As soon as he was finished, he would brainstorm how to find Emma.

Or maybe he should brainstorm how to win her back. Perhaps his time would be better spent wooing her rather than searching for her, especially when he had no clue where to start.

She would eventually call someone. She had to.

A name card fell from his hand to the floor when Elliot pulled out his phone, his facial expression turning into terror.

Something happened, and it didn't look like anything good.

He met Elliot halfway across the ballroom, his stomach twisting like someone was taking a knife and jamming it into him repeatedly.

"Officer Stockman found her vehicle in the middle of the road heading out of town. It was empty."

He shook his head, confused. "Empty? What does that mean?"

"Maybe she got a ride back to town from someone."

"Why didn't she call me? Or you? Or Lynn? Or Theresa? Or—"

"Take a deep breath, Bentley. She's okay."

His expression hardened. "You don't know that. Maybe she's not."

"Well, I refuse to dwell on the negative, so I'm going with she's okay." Elliot nodded toward the exit. "I want to check out her car myself. Do you want to come with?"

He glanced quickly at Daphne, who nodded once with a smile. She was giving her okay that he could leave. He gave a nod back, but honestly, he would've left without her blessing.

Emma was too important.

They made it to her vehicle fifteen minutes later. She hadn't made it that far out of town, about two miles before her vehicle must've died on her. The keys were still in the ignition.

That worried him. Why would she leave the keys?

Unless someone took her against her will.

Did Jared come back into town and hurt her?

He'd kill him if he touched one hair on her head.

"Wally tried starting the car before he hooked it up to the tow truck. It's definitely dead. I didn't see anyone walking on the side of the road heading this way. Officer Johnson drove a few miles heading out of town to make sure she wasn't walking that way. So we're assuming she must've gotten a ride from someone," Officer Stockman said, as if he was rattling off a random report to the chief of police.

But nothing about this was random.

This was personal.

This was about Emma.

Even Elliot looked like he was trembling with nerves, and not from the cold weather or the snow falling preciously to the ground, like a beautiful white blanket trying to wrap them up and comfort them somehow.

"Something happened. She didn't call anyone and she left the damn keys in the car!" Bentley whipped a hand at the vehicle attached to the tow truck as he shouted.

"We can't automatically assume something bad happened," Elliot said quietly, probably trying to calm him down using a low tone of voice, but it did nothing but further rankle his anger.

He was angry.

Feeling angry felt so much better than letting the intense fear consume him.

"Maybe Jared's back."

There. He said it. How would Elliot react?

Surprisingly, Elliot nodded. "I'll contact Robertsville and ask if their department will do a check for me. If he did do something, we'll find out. I will find Emma." Elliot stepped closer. "Take my truck, go home, and try not to worry. I'll find her."

"I can't—"

"You can, and you will." Elliot's intense expression said he wouldn't be winning the argument.

"But—"

"No buts. Go."

He wanted to scream. He wanted to throw the tantrum of all tantrums.

In the end, he conceded like a man in control when he felt like he was spinning precariously on a ride ready to fall off.

He drove home slowly, not wanting to enter the darkness, the loneliness. If something happened to—

No. He had to stop thinking negatively. If Elliot could

think positively when he had to be going out of his mind with worry, then so could he.

Twisting the key in the lock, he realized his door was already unlocked. His mind had been so frazzled since the fight with Emma, he didn't lock the door when he left.

Did it matter if anyone broke in? They could steal every last thing he owned. None of it mattered as long as Emma was okay.

Slamming the door shut, he tore off his jacket and threw it to the ground.

Focus on the anger, not the fear.

That's all he needed to do.

He could use a punching bag right about now.

"What happened? Are you okay?"

His head jerked to the sweet, beautiful sound of Emma's voice.

She slowly stood up from the couch and took a step toward him, then stopped.

Every terrible, crushing emotion that had inhabited his body since seeing her car abandoned in the middle of the road vanished.

All replaced with relief. A profound sense of relief.

He made it to her in three long strides and wrapped her into his arms so tightly he heard her sharp intake of breath.

He was never letting her go.

Never.

She wasn't sure why Bentley was acting so strangely, mad one second, almost—relieved—the next. But his warm embrace was already heating her cold, numb body up.

The walk from her dead car to his home had frozen her

straight to the bone. He had a fireplace, and if she would've known how to start a fire without lighting the entire house in flames, she would've.

"Bentley..."

She didn't know where to start. An apology? A confession?

He buried his head into the crook of her neck, his hot breath, his warm embrace, helping to soothe a little more of the icicles running through her veins.

"I thought something happened to you. We found your car...the keys...don't leave." He pulled away and clamped his hands hard onto her shoulders. "Don't ever leave again. Whatever you think, you're wrong. You belong here. With me."

"I know."

"So you can't leave. Do you—" His grim expression froze as his eyes widened. "What did you say?"

"I know where I belong. I..." She let out a small breath, then eyed his left hand. "I like your hands on me, but not when they're digging in."

He relaxed his grip with a silly grin. That sweet, sexy, adorable grin filled up more of her aching heart that had grappled with a decision so painfully the last hour. He grabbed her hand and pulled her to the couch. They sat down together.

"Your hands are like icicles. What happened, Emma? Talk to me. Real talk."

"I was going to leave. I was going to run once again. When something bad or difficult happens in my life, it's so much easier to ignore it. And then my car died. It's as if it knew I couldn't leave."

"That's one smart car. It's going to get the best damn engine I can find."

She laughed as his goofy grin widened. "I'm scared, Bentley. I'm—"

"You have nothing to be scared about. I'm not mad. I'm the one who is sorry."

"Let me finish." She squeezed his hand tightly, needing some of his strength she felt pulsing through his body. Or was it tremors of fear that she would leave again? "I'm broke. I'm jobless, if you don't count the bakery. I have no background in anything. But I..."

"What? Tell me."

"Well, I'm not even close to an expert with graphic design, but I think Lynn could branch out and sell things online. Create a website and make a lot more money with her delicious treats."

"And it sounds like you could help her. You're not dumb, Emma."

She pursed her lips playfully, yet with a serious glint in her eyes. "You're interrupting."

A crooked grin touched his lips.

"I'm homeless. I have no family left. I feel so lost in life and I don't know where to go." Her eyes tried to express how much these next words truly meant. "And then I met you and life made sense. But I'm still scared. I don't want to rely on you. I don't want to be a burden. I want to make it on my own." She leaned forward and squeezed his hands even harder. "But I don't want to leave you either."

"Can I talk yet?" His gorgeous smile melted more of her frozen heart.

"Seems like you already are. You never listen."

His smile disappeared. "You're right, when it counts, I don't. You might not have said you were hurting, but I didn't listen to your unspoken words. We should've had this kind of talk ages ago."

"Bentley, we've known each other for, like, two weeks. It really hasn't been that long. We shouldn't even feel the way we do."

"And yet, I love you."

She inhaled a sharp breath. "You can't possibly—"

"Yep. I do." He pressed his lips to hers before she could protest again. The kiss was slow and sweet and told her with a gentle caress how much he truly loved her. He sat back. "Did you walk from your car to my house?"

She nodded, unable to express why. She needed time to think, to sort through all the problems rolling around her mind. Strangely enough, the long, brutal, cold walk helped her. She saw everything so clearly when she reached his house.

When she realized he left the house unlocked, she knew they could work through anything, because he trusted her enough to come back on her own. He didn't lock her out. Now, she knew he didn't lock her out of his heart either.

"Why did you leave the keys in the ignition? I thought...I thought something bad happened. Truly bad."

"I didn't mean to scare anyone. The car's dead. It's a goner. It's not coming back to life. I didn't think it mattered if I left the keys in there."

Her heart started to quiver with unease when his sweet smile vanished, his eyebrows puckered into a frown. Then it started to tremble with anguish when he let go of her hands and stood up.

"I'll be right back. I have to call Elliot. He's got a search party going for you."

He walked out of the room.

What? Why did he walk away?

She felt like she was on the cusp of a happy reunion,

laying her heart on the line, telling him things she never shared with anyone. Her deep, dark fears.

None of it mattered to him.

He didn't want her.

What was all that talk about love? If he loved her, he wouldn't have walked away.

Well, it's a good thing she didn't profess her love back.

She at least saved herself from embarrassment.

19

Running a hand through his hair, then pulling on the ends, he groaned in frustration. He needed something amazing, something so spectacular she would never think about leaving again. He had about one minute to come up with that one thing that would secure her into his future.

She felt like a burden, when she was a fresh of breath air. Every time he saw a sweet smile shine upon her beautiful face, his heart lit up with joy. Every time she gazed at him with desire so strong she could rip his clothes off in the middle of the bar, or wherever they happened to be, his heart pounded with lust. Every time she brushed a tender hand across his body, letting him know more wonderful touches were to come, his heart splintered into a love so profound he couldn't wait for the next soft touch.

She was his everything, and yet he could lose her by saying or doing the wrong thing. She walked miles in the cold weather, with the snow coming down, without calling one person.

She wanted to do everything on her own.

And he wanted to do it all for her.

What a dilemma.

An idea suddenly warped his brain and refused to leave. Digging into the top drawer of his dresser where he kept anything and everything—his junk drawer of his bedroom—he found what he was looking for and then walked back to the living room.

Emma was pacing from one end of the couch to the other.

"What did Elliot say?"

Elliot?

Oh, yeah, he called him. How did he forget about that?

"He's glad to know you're okay. He said to call him." He smiled, hoping to ease the concern coating her eyes. "But I need something from you first."

"To get the hell out. No problem."

Blocking her exit, he forced his smile to stay in place. He wouldn't let her erratic moods, which he now saw as a defense mechanism, stop him from his crazy plan.

Absolutely crazy.

"Who said I wanted you to leave?"

"You said—"

"That I needed something from you. I didn't specify what."

Cocking a brow, still maintaining her fight or flight mode, she rolled her hand in a gesture for him to continue.

"You still owe me a Christmas wish." A slow grin emerged. "Remember, when we played cards and you lost? I'm cashing in on my Christmas wish."

"Now?"

"Right now."

"But...I thought you wanted me gone."

Grabbing her by the shoulders, he tried to keep his

hands loose, but failed. "Get that out of your head. I don't want you to leave. I have never once said it. Not once. I just told you I love you. Get it to sink in."

Her hands grabbed his and pulled them down, then she linked fingers with him. A heavy breath escaped. "I'm trying here, Bentley. I can't help it. My emotions are haywire."

"I know. Mine, too."

A tentative smile touched her lips. "Okay. What's your Christmas wish?"

Letting go of one hand, he dug into his pocket and then pulled his hand out and made a fist. He held it out to her. "Open your hand."

She eyed his fist warily. "What's in your hand?"

"It doesn't matter. It could be anything."

She stared at his fist as if she stared hard enough she'd find the meaning of life.

"Take a leap of faith, Emma. It shouldn't matter what's in my hand, but you know it's from me. And I love you. This is my Christmas wish. I wish you would trust me and know that I love you no matter what."

"I've lost so much in life. I'm afraid of losing you, too. My fear controls me more than I care to admit."

"Yet, you just admitted it. That's one step closer to overcoming it. Will you grant me this wish? Open your hand."

She let go of his hand. He suppressed the smile that wanted to break free from how hard she had clung to his hand, squeezing, almost crushing his bones. But she let go, and she now had her hand raised between them. Except, she was still letting her fear win.

"You have to open your hand."

A shaky laugh escaped. "This is silly."

"I won the game, and I want my wish. You can't go back on your word."

Her expression stiffened, yet the glee in her eyes said he hit the right nerve. She would never negate on her word.

Her hand slowly loosened until her palm was face up and waiting patiently for him. "There. It's open."

He smiled as he placed his hand over hers and dropped a key into her palm.

She looked at the key intensely, probably running scenario after scenario in her head. It looked like any normal key. To a house. To a lock. To a car. To a shed. A plain old key. If he wanted to get philosophical...to his heart.

"What's this for? I don't get it. Is your wish granted? Are we done?" She chuckled.

"Yep." His smile grew as he laughed with her.

"That's it?" She shoved him lightly as her laughter built. "Come on, tell me what it's for."

He snaked a hand around her waist and touched her lips gently as he whispered, "To my house. You need your own key. Because I'm not letting you leave. And just so you know, the key wasn't my wish."

Then his tongue dove in and staked claim. She didn't fight him as her arms wove around his neck. He heard the key fall softly to the wooden floor.

He tried to tell her how much he loved her by kissing her soft and sweet, then rough and hard. Just like their tumultuous relationship. Nothing between them was ever the same when they interacted. At times, they were light and carefree, and at other times, sparring like two warriors to the death. He wouldn't take her any other way.

Life would definitely never be boring.

Coaxing a delectable moan from her, the kiss then turned tender, soothing all her worries with the touch of his lips. If it didn't work this time, he'd keep kissing her until it did. He'd never stop.

The kiss slowed and stopped.

Her hands tightened around his neck. "If the key wasn't the wish, then what was?"

"Your trust. Your faith in me. You had no idea what was in my hand, if anything even was, yet you held it out for me. That's all I wanted." He pressed his forehead to hers. "Was that the cheesiest thing that's ever happened? Because now I'm thinking that was pretty lame. Can we have a do over? I want this to be romantic." *Like the mistletoe thing Aiden did for Theresa.* Although, he didn't say that out loud.

Her hands slid up his neck and through his hair. A soft, sweet caress that made him ache for more. "This is the most romantic thing that's ever happened to me. You managed to calm my racing nerves and convince me you love me all in one gesture." She giggled. "Or maybe it was the kiss, because that fear is creeping back in."

"Well, we can't have that." He swept her into his arms. A happy squeal punctured the room as she wrapped her arms around him. "To the bedroom, my fair lady, for more kisses of cheesiness."

Her laughter rang through the house as he made his way down the hallway. "That made no sense, Bentley." Her head rested against his chest as she snuggled closer. "Yet, it made perfect sense. I love you, too."

He kissed her head as he inhaled her sweet scent. A mixture of berry, sugar, and oddly enough, sweat. She smelled like the bakery, but with hard work mixed in.

"Just so we're clear, no more running. If you have an issue, we talk it out. We can turn it into a pillow fight or something equally crazy if it helps."

She lifted her head. "For every sentence, we get to swing the pillow at each other."

"Exactly." He tossed her on the bed and grabbed a pillow.

She immediately took up her defense and grabbed the other pillow, kneeling on the bed with an eager, yet determined expression on her face.

The beauty before him almost dropped him to his knees. She couldn't get more beautiful if she tried. But she did. Every single day. Every single minute. Every single second.

"I'm sorry for running and scaring you." She swung the pillow, connecting with his chest as a giggle escaped and she retreated.

He took aim. "I forgive you and will make you pay with too many kisses." He swung the pillow and hit her stomach.

"I love you and will always talk things out." The pillow hit him in the head softly.

He chuckled as he took another light swing at her. "I love you, too, and will spank your ass for every time you don't talk it out."

Then he dropped the pillow and relished in her happy scream as he dove on the bed and wrapped her in his embrace. Settling perfectly on her body, he dipped down and stole a kiss.

"Best Christmas wish I ever got."

20

Warm breath tickled her neck, then Bentley's lips followed.

"Is that a tear I see lingering in the corner of your eye?"

Swiping a hand at her eye, she laid a hand on his thigh and lightly squeezed. "Behave. There are no tears. You're supposed to be quiet."

She glanced around the church at all the smiling faces as they gazed upon Daphne, who looked beautiful. She hated to admit that, but after digging deep last night, she realized it wasn't so much a problem with Daphne she had. It was what she embodied. That happiness she could never quite grasp. That was never quite within her reach.

As Bentley laid a hand over hers that rested tenderly on his thigh, she knew happiness had finally touched her.

It was in her reach.

She didn't need to feel threatened by this woman, which was why she dressed this morning for a wedding she never had any intention of attending.

The smile and appreciation on Bentley's face had been worth it.

And no, she was most definitely not crying. Why would she cry? It was a dumb wedding.

He linked fingers with her, then raised her hand to his mouth for a light kiss. Then he bent his head toward her again, his lips finding the same spot from before. The kiss melted her senses and filled her heart with so much joy she swore she would burst at any moment.

"I love you. I just thought I'd say that."

This was why she wanted to cry.

Because Bentley was so sweet and caring. The perfect guy.

She wanted to be standing up in front of the altar across from him, dressed all in white, and saying vows she thought she'd never say. That feeling definitely fortified deep inside her this morning when he gave her an early Christmas present. Wrapped in a tiny red box with a silver bow on top, she couldn't believe her eyes when she opened it.

A heart shaped locket. Not just any silly old locket to wear around her neck that expressed their love. But the perfect gift she would've never dreamed of in her life.

He put a picture of her dad and mom on each side, so they would always be with her. That was the most sweetest, caring thing anyone could have done for her. The moment he placed it around her neck, she felt more alive, more whole than she had since her father passed away. It felt as if they were right there with her. She didn't even ask him how he managed to get a picture of her parents. With Bentley, it simply didn't surprise her. When he wanted something, he got it.

He got her.

The present she had for him was lame compared to

what he gave her. She only bought him a pair of Christmas boxers that said "Jingle my balls," knowing he'd get a good laugh out of it, which he did. Her ideas failed after that on what else to get him. Then, last night, before they went to bed, she ordered two tickets to see his favorite band three months from now. A sign, a gesture of her trust that she wouldn't be leaving any time soon, because she'd be attending that concert with him. It put a serious dent into her measly savings, but it had been worth every penny.

The morning had been filled with love and laughter, and so much merriness. They were almost late to the ceremony when they showed their thanks to one another.

"What is that beautiful mind of yours thinking? Care to share?"

"You're not supposed to talk in church." A low giggle escaped as his lips touched her neck once again.

"I can't help myself." He brought their joined hands to his lap. "You look beautiful today."

Pressing her lips together to keep the giddy smile off her face, she decided to let it go. If he wanted to keep whispering adoring, loving words to her, why should she stop him? She wanted to hear them.

"Thanks for coming with. I know you probably—"

She turned and pressed her lips to his, cutting off whatever he thought about her feelings toward Daphne. Whispering against his lips, she said, "I'm sorry for my attitude toward her. Daphne isn't that bad." She moved away, then bit her bottom lip. "It's still weird she's getting married on Christmas Eve."

Bentley chuckled, then looked bashful as Elliot turned around in front of them and gave both of them a stern look that said they had better stop talking.

They both pressed their lips together to stop from laughing, then settled quietly to watch the rest of the ceremony. Twenty minutes later, they were following the crowd out of the church and heading to the reception.

When she found her name at the same table as Bentley, Aiden, Theresa, and Theresa's brother, she didn't hide the surprise from her face.

"I had hoped you'd show up with Bentley."

Turning around, a hand went to her chest, startled. Daphne had a gentle smile on her face. She still couldn't understand how someone could smile all day, every day. Didn't it get tiresome?

But maybe she could learn a thing or two from Daphne. Learn how to keep that happiness front and center. Something she obviously needed to work on.

"It was a beautiful ceremony. Congrats." She looked away. "Sorry about..." She shrugged and glanced back at her. "You know, my attitude."

Daphne's smile didn't waver. "Friends?"

Emma matched her smile, displaying a real one. "I'd like that."

Daphne squealed excitedly and grabbed a hug. "Me, too. Bentley's a great guy. I'm so happy for you two."

They talked a few more minutes and then Daphne ventured off to another couple to talk and spread her joy.

Plopping down in her chair, she sat for a moment. To appreciate how wonderful her life had turned. She left her small town lost, confused, and feeling so alone, only to find this magical small town that made her feel welcomed, accepted, and oh so beautiful.

Well, mostly Bentley made her feel beautiful.

A genuine smile touched her lips as Elliot and Lynn approached her. Nerves also attacked because she hadn't yet apologized for scaring everyone yesterday. Something she hadn't meant to do.

Standing up, she didn't stop to ask or even question her actions. She wrapped her arms around Elliot and squeezed tightly, as if she could take some of his kindness and fill herself up.

His arms enveloped her back. "I'm glad you're sticking around."

Even when he should be berating her for creating such a fiasco last night, he had to say things that she didn't deserve.

Letting go slowly, she forced herself to look him in the eye. "I'm sorry for scaring everyone yesterday. I never meant to do that."

"It's a new day. It's Christmas Eve, and it's going to be a great day. Don't worry about it. Are you and Bentley still coming over later?" Elliot asked, the hopefulness etched across his face.

"Definitely." She snapped her fingers, then started to rummage through her purse until she found the bright red envelope and held it out to them. "This is for both of you. It's my Christmas present to you. It's not much, but..." She shrugged. "I hope you like it."

It wasn't exactly the idea Theresa and Aiden helped her come up with, but she thought it was the best gift she could give them.

"It's not what the present is, it's the thought behind it." Lynn's smile said she believed every word of that.

Elliot and Lynn shared a tender look, then Lynn took the envelope from her. Opening it slowly, as if treasuring the silly envelope like it was a big box wrapped in glittering paper, she took her time.

"She opens everything like this." Elliot chuckled as he

tossed a loving arm around Lynn, who giggled and finally opened the flap of the envelope.

Lynn pulled out a card. Silence ensued as they both read the contents, and then Lynn's mouth dropped into a circle as Elliot's eyes lit up with pleasure.

"This is extremely kind of you, Emma," he said, laying a hand on Lynn's belly.

"Well, I'm no baby expert, but I do know you'll need breaks and stuff. I'm more than happy to help out."

When she asked Theresa and Aiden for help in finding the perfect present for Elliot and Lynn, claiming her Christmas wish from them, they suggested things she could buy that would've made both of them happy. But she was still working hard and trying to save up money. She didn't have a lot of money to spend this year on presents. Although, she made sure she bought something for Laura, a makeup kit that she hoped Lynn didn't hate her for, and two fun Christmas shirts for Gregory and Gabby that would put a smile on their faces.

Next year she'd have more money to go crazy.

But when the idea to make a coupon book full of babysitting vouchers popped in her head, she knew right away it was the best present she could give Lynn and Elliot. They would need a babysitter when the baby got here. Everyone needed a break on occasion. She'd do it free of charge and whenever they needed her.

A tear slid down Lynn's face as she grabbed a hug. "This is such a beautiful present. Thank you so much." Lynn hugged her tighter. "Honestly, it's the best present. Because when I had Laura, I was all alone. I never had a break."

Warmth spread throughout her heart and filled her soul. She finally managed to get one thing right. She could've almost whooped with joy.

Elliot joined the hug and they all laughed. Shortly after, they walked away.

Before she could sit down and enjoy a moment to herself, Bentley stopped in front of her, swooped an arm around her waist, and pulled her in for a kiss.

A kiss as sweet as a cup of hot chocolate filled to the rim with tiny white marshmallows. And just as hot as one. Sweet, hot, and with a hint of peppermint.

The taste of peppermint made her giggle. "Did you eat a candy cane?"

"I just took a candy cane shot."

"Isn't it a little early for that?"

"It's a celebration." He picked her up and twirled her. A loud, joyous giggle erupted. He set her down gently. "There's a lot to celebrate."

"Besides Daphne's wedding?"

A crooked grin appeared. "That's right."

"What else are we celebrating?"

Another minty kiss hit her lips. "The most beautiful woman is in my arms. What else?" He winked.

"Stop getting sweeter and sweeter. It's not right."

"I'm absolutely terrible. I'll stop this minute." Then he grabbed her hand and pulled her onto the dance floor. "Now dance with me."

And she did.

He swirled her around the dance floor. Made her laugh. Made her smile. Made her feel precious.

Even though it felt strange to be celebrating a wedding on Christmas Eve, it was the best wedding she had ever attended.

She also knew this would be the best Christmas she ever had.

Don't miss the rest of the books in this heartwarming holiday series!

Merry Me
Mistletoe Magic
Snowed in Love
Snowflakes and Shots
Holiday Hope

For Elliot & Lynn's story
Merry Me
A Holiday Romance Novel - Book 1

He never knew a simple gift left on his porch step would mend his wounded heart.

Hiding his dislike for the holidays isn't easy, especially when Chief Elliot Duncan meets a woman who captures his attention with one sweet smile. Lynn Carpenter is beautiful, strong-willed, and hardworking, and he doesn't know how to return her gift that was left on his porch by mistake. As Christmas approaches, it doesn't take much for the holiday spirit to seep in, not when Lynn makes it so effortless with her excitement. The only thing he wants for Christmas this year is her heart. But between his meddling father and the need to take care of her, something she passionately resists, he knows it won't be that simple. He's up for the challenge, because losing Lynn is unacceptable.

For Aiden & Theresa's story
Mistletoe Magic
A Holiday Romance Novel - Book 2

A mistletoe. A kiss. This just might be the start of a beautiful Christmas.

Theresa might not make the best pot of coffee in town, but people still flock to the diner for a cup, even Officer Crowl, who rarely displays a smile since his fiancé died. She'll never be able to win his heart, but it's hard to resist him, especially when he kisses her under the mistletoe. Well, on the cheek, but that has to count for something...right?

Staying busy keeps Officer Aiden Crowl sane. Because when he's idle or alone, he thinks, and nothing good comes from that. Everyone thinks he's the perfect man. They think he's broken because she's gone. He is, just not for the reason they believe. Every time he walks into the diner, one sweet smile from Theresa erases some of the pain. He should stay away from her. Far away. But what is he supposed to do when they're standing under a mistletoe? Kiss her, of course.

For James & Erin's story

Snowed in Love

A Holiday Romance Novel - Book 4

A blizzard. A cabin. A cup of hot chocolate.
The perfect mixture to fall in love.

James Brennen is nothing but a screwup. At least, in the small town of Mulberry, that's what everyone thinks of him. As a recovering alcoholic, he's trying his best to turn his life around, to be a better man. All of his hard work comes crashing down when he's fired from his job at the hospital—accused of stealing drugs. Nothing ever changes and he's done trying to prove himself. Needing time alone, his friend's cabin in the middle of the woods provides the perfect escape. He knows he's found deep trouble, not only when he gets stranded during a brutal snowstorm, but that he's stuck with the one woman he's wanted since the first day he laid eyes on her. The passion burns bright between them, but it doesn't matter, because as soon as Christmas is over, he's leaving for good.

For Stu & Chasity's story

Snowflakes and Shots

A Holiday Romance Novel - Book 5

One last shot at love...

Stu doesn't have many regrets in life—not even the fact he never decorates his bar for the holidays. But when a bar fight turns into needing medical attention, he's put face-to-face with the one woman he's tried to avoid for the last fifteen years. Okay, so maybe he regrets a few things. He should've never walked away from her. It only took a good knock to his head to make him see clearly. He's going to win Chasity's heart once again. It doesn't matter that she's not going to make it easy; he's up for the challenge. Bring on the bets and all the Christmas spirit he can handle. Except, one person doesn't like the idea of them together—the same person that had him walking away from her all those years ago.

ABOUT THE AUTHOR

I'm a *USA Today* Bestselling Author that loves to write sweet contemporary romance and romantic suspense novels, although I am partial to romantic suspense. Honestly, I love anything that has to do with romance. As long as there's a happy ending, I'm a happy camper. And insta-love...yes, please! I love baseball (Go Twins!) and creating awesome crafts. I graduated with a Bachelor's Degree in Criminal Justice, working in that field for several years before I became a stay-at-home mom. I have a few more amazing stories in the works. If you would like to connect with me or see important news, head to my website at http://www.amandasiegrist.com. Thanks for reading!

Made in the USA
Las Vegas, NV
30 November 2023

81860837R00129